## *"What do you want?" Tanner's voice was just short of a bark.*

"I'm not sure," Anna said honestly. "I thought you might need something."

He took a step forward, leaving the shadows of his bedroom. Now she could see the darkness in his eyes, feel the dangerous energy that rolled off him. She was acutely aware of the bed mere inches from where she stood.

"And just what was it you thought I might need?" he asked, his voice laced with a weary edge.

Her mouth dried and her heart began to pound. She took a step toward him. "I think you need me to be here with you."

Tanner's eyes narrowed and she felt the taut, powerful energy of him sweeping over her, warning her. "Anna, if you don't leave now, this cowboy won't be responsible for the consequences."

Dear Reader,

Love is in the air, but the days will certainly be sweeter if you snuggle up with this month's Silhouette Intimate Moments offerings (and a heart-shaped box of decadent chocolates) and let yourself go on the ride of your life! First up, veteran Carla Cassidy dazzles us with *Protecting the Princess*, part of her new miniseries WILD WEST BODYGUARDS. Here, a rugged cowboy rescues a princess and whisks her off to his ranch. What a way to go…!

RITA® Award-winning author Catherine Mann sets our imaginations on fire when she throws together two unlikely lovers in *Explosive Alliance*, the latest book in her popular WINGMEN WARRIORS miniseries. In *Stolen Memory*, the fourth book in her TROUBLE IN EDEN miniseries, stellar storyteller Virginia Kantra tells the tale of a beautiful police officer who sets out to uncover the cause of a powerful man's amnesia. But this supersleuth never expects to fall in love! The second book in her LAST CHANCE HEROES miniseries, *Truly, Madly, Dangerously* by Linda Winstead Jones, plunges us into the lives of a feisty P.I. and protective deputy sheriff who find romance while solving a grisly murder.

Lorna Michaels will touch readers with *Stranger in Her Arms*, in which a caring heroine tends to a rain-battered stranger who shows up on her doorstep. And *Warrior Without a Cause* by Nancy Gideon features a special agent who takes charge when a stalking victim needs his help…and his love.

You won't want to miss this array of roller-coaster reads from Intimate Moments—the line that delivers a charge and a satisfying finish you're sure to savor.

Happy Valentine's Day!

Patience Smith
Associate Senior Editor

Please address questions and book requests to:
Silhouette Reader Service
U.S.: 3010 Walden Ave., P.O. Box 1325, Buffalo, NY 14269
Canadian: P.O. Box 609, Fort Erie, Ont. L2A 5X3

# Protecting
# the Princess

## CARLA CASSIDY

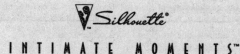

INTIMATE MOMENTS™

Published by Silhouette Books

America's Publisher of Contemporary Romance

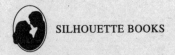 SILHOUETTE BOOKS

ISBN 0-373-27415-7

PROTECTING THE PRINCESS

Visit Silhouette Books at www.eHarlequin.com

**Printed in U.S.A.**

**Books by Carla Cassidy**

# CARLA CASSIDY

is an award-winning author who has written over fifty books for Silhouette. In 1995, she won Best Silhouette Romance from *Romantic Times* for *Anything for Danny*. In 1998, she also won a Career Achievement Award for Best Innovative Series from *Romantic Times*.

Carla believes the only thing better than curling up with a good book to read is sitting down at the computer with a good story to write. She's looking forward to writing many more books and bringing hours of pleasure to readers.

# *Prologue*

The explosion of gunfire shattered the beauty of the California spring morning. Screams rent the air as people dove for cover or ran blindly in terror.

It happened so quickly she didn't have a chance to do anything but react. Princess Anna Johansson and her father, King Bjorn Johansson had just retrieved their baggage and been heading out of the Los Angeles airport to hail a cab when a pair of men opened fire.

The air filled with the acrid smoke of danger. A panicked crowd jostled Anna away from the scene as they pushed and shoved to escape. She dropped her suitcase in an effort to stay on her feet as the people went wild.

She held tightly to her purse and small overnight bag despite the press of the bodies against her.

Panic choked her as she lost sight of her father in the resulting chaos. What was happening? Had he been shot? How had they been found? They had been traveling under different names, had changed planes twice in the past twenty-four hours. How had the rebels known where they were?

Anna managed to slip out of the crowd that carried her away and crouch behind a stack of luggage. She tried to see what was happening, tried to catch sight of her father.

Her heart thundered. She had to go back. She had to find her father. But fear kept her momentarily rooted in place. What if they'd killed him? Grief ripped through her, but it was a grief that couldn't be sustained beneath the weight of cold, stark fear.

What if the gunmen were still around the area? They wouldn't be satisfied just killing her father. As his only heir, she was a liability.

Her heart continued its rapid beat as she tried to make sense of what had just occurred. She'd thought when they reached the United States they'd be safe. They had been so careful with their travel plans.

Roused from their beds two nights prior to the sound of gunfire and explosions, they'd learned from loyal palace staff members that rebels had taken over the small island kingdom.

Their lives in danger, they'd been hustled away

from the palace and into hiding until arrangements had been made to get them out of the country.

At this moment none of that mattered. What mattered was finding her father and getting them both to someplace safe. But, where was safe? And where was her father?

Taking a deep breath as she left the cover of the luggage stack, she tried to head back in the direction where she and her father had been separated, but was halted by police before she could even get close to the area.

There was no way she could speak to the authorities. She was traveling with false identification. She had no idea what might happen if she was detained. Her father had warned her that there would be danger until he could speak with the appropriate people and request some sort of temporary asylum. She had no idea who she could trust.

Think. She had to think. Turning away from the police line, she inhaled several more deep breaths in an attempt to still the racing of her heart. Her father had planned for the possibility of trouble.

Aware that her life could still be in danger, she hailed a cab and slid into the back seat.

"Take me to the nearest hotel," she said to the driver, then slumped back in the seat to catch her breath. The past forty-eight hours had been terrifying and apparently the danger wasn't behind her yet.

She wouldn't actually check in to a hotel, but she

could sit in the lobby to take a few minutes to bring her nerves under control and hopefully catch a news report to see exactly what had happened.

Digging into her purse, she withdrew the business card her father had handed her just before their plane had landed. "If there is trouble…" he'd said. "If we get separated for any reason, you go here."

He'd handed her the little white card that read "Wild West Protective Services." She had noted the address in Cotter Creek, Oklahoma, and several telephone numbers as he'd added. "These people will protect you and I will join you there as soon as it is possible."

She held the card tightly between her fingers and stared at it. Wild West Protective Services. She had no desire to go to Cotter Creek, Oklahoma, but knew she had no other choice.

She was in a strange country, with nothing more than what was contained in her purse and small overnight bag. Separated from her father, she would only be able to rejoin him if she got to Cotter Creek and utilized the services of these Wild West bodyguards.

She only prayed that the attack hadn't left her father dead and that the assassins wouldn't find her before her father did.

# Chapter 1

"You must protect me." The voice belonged to the attractive blonde who flew through the open door of the Wild West Protective Services office.

Slamming the door, she locked it, then leaned against it as if to bar the hounds of hell from bursting through behind her.

Tanner West had just been about to leave the office for the day, but a burst of adrenaline drove all thoughts of home out of his head. Unsure of what was going on, he grabbed the 9 mm gun that was never far from his reach.

"Protect you from who?" Unceremoniously pushing her aside, he was fully aware that a lock on a door wouldn't keep out somebody determined to get in.

"You don't have to get physical," the blonde exclaimed, apparently offended by his actions.

He ignored her protest as he peered out the window. Nothing. He saw nobody on the street who looked like any kind of a threat. "What am I looking for?" he asked. "Who is after you? A crazy husband? A jealous boyfriend? A homicidal boss?"

"Rebel assassins."

He whirled from the window to stare at her, wondering if perhaps she was pulling his leg.

Rebel assassins in Cotter Creek?

She was a stranger to him. In a town the size of Cotter Creek, Oklahoma, he knew almost everyone and he'd never seen her before in his life. She was the type of woman he'd remember. "Rebel assassins?"

She nodded and dropped the small overnight bag she'd carried in to the floor. "Although I'm hoping I lost them after the shoot-out at the airport in Los Angeles."

Tanner felt as if he'd been thrust into the middle of a movie and had no idea of the beginning so couldn't begin to guess at the ending. Was the pretty blonde in front of him in need of some kind of protection or was she in the throes of some paranoid delusion?

"Maybe we should start at the beginning," he said, gesturing her toward the chair in front of the reception desk.

"I'm Tanner West, CEO of Wild West Protective Services." She sat in the chair and he moved to sit behind the desk—setting his gun next to him where it could be grabbed in a split second if needed. He took advantage of the moment to look at her more closely.

Her features were dainty. Her eyes a clear blue and her hair long and golden. Just looking at her caused the slightest rise in his pulse. She was one knockout.

"My father sent me here. Six nights ago rebel forces took over our palace and we fled our country and got on a plane for the United States. My father told me on the flight that if there was trouble, if for some reason we got separated, I was to come here to Cotter Creek and seek your aid. Obviously there was trouble, otherwise I wouldn't be here now. My father instructed me to come here and said you'd take care of things until he could arrive here, as well."

As his sense of urgency fled an edge of impatience took its place. He was no more clear now about what was going on than he'd been moments before when she'd first burst through the office door.

"Are you going to tell me who you are? Who your father is?" he asked, unable to keep the impatience from his voice.

Her startling blue eyes flashed with what appeared to be a touch of impatience of her own and her dainty chin rose slightly. "I am Princess Anna Johansson from the Island of Niflheim."

Tanner sat straighter in his chair, a new urgency

slicing through him. "Your father is King Bjorn?" Tanner had met the king of the small Scandinavian country two months before at a fund-raiser in Washington, D.C. At that time the king had mentioned having a twenty-five-year-old daughter. "Where is your father now?"

Her eyes darkened. "I don't know. We got separated at the airport in Los Angeles. Gunmen were waiting for us when we walked out of the exit to find ground transportation. The only thing I know for sure is that he wasn't shot. The news reports right after the incident indicated, thankfully, that nobody had been hurt but the suspects had gotten away."

She had a smoky kind of voice, a smooth alto that under other circumstances he might have found sexy as hell. But sex was the last thing on his mind at this moment.

He'd caught a bit of a newscast concerning the shooting at LAX and now wished he'd paid more attention, because it appeared that he'd just been handed the biggest protection assignment of his career. An assignment that would solidify Wild West Protective Services as the premier agency to call when trouble came knocking.

He and his father had been following the news report on the coup, although the information coming out of the small country had been sketchy. He hadn't realized until this moment that the incident at the airport and the coup in Niflheim were related, as the reporters had apparently not realized that King Bjorn and his daughter had been in the airport melee.

If her story was true, and he had no reason to doubt it, then the most urgent need was to get her to a safe location.

He stood and grabbed his black Stetson cowboy hat from the top of the file cabinet. "Come on. We've got to get you out of here."

She got up from the chair, her gaze focused upward on his hat as a tiny frown appeared across her forehead. "Are you a cowboy?"

She said the word with the same inflection she might have used to say "ax murderer." "Among other things," he answered. "We need to go." He had no idea what problem she might have with cowboys, but he didn't have time for it right now. His initial thought was to get her someplace safe immediately.

"Where are you taking me?" She leaned down to pick up the small overnight bag, then held it out for him to carry.

He grabbed the bag and headed for the front door. "To the ranch."

"The ranch?" She halted all forward movement, a new frown tugging together her pale, perfectly arched eyebrows. "Oh, that won't do. I don't do ranches. Surely there's a nice hotel here in town. What I'd really like is a long massage. The past two days on that bus were an absolute nightmare."

Tanner stared at her in disbelief. She'd just told him

that rebel assassins were after her, and she was worried about whether she could get a massage or not. He recognized at that moment that the princess might be pretty and sexy as all get-out, but she just might be trouble, as well.

"Look, lady, right now my goal is to get you someplace safe. You might have to skip a massage or two to stay alive."

Her vivid blue eyes narrowed. "There's no reason to use that tone of voice with me, Mr. West."

Tanner bit back his aggravation. "Your father sent you here for safekeeping and until I have a better idea of what's going on, the safest place for you to be is at the family ranch." He wasn't about to let her screw this up for him by making unrealistic demands.

He moved to the door, unlocked it and eased it open, his gun once again in hand. He simply didn't have enough information yet to know how imminent the danger might be for her.

The late-afternoon April sun shone on the quiet streets of the small town. Two women walked at a leisurely pace up the sidewalk and old man Thompson sat in a wooden chair outside his barbershop waiting for customers. There was nothing to indicate assassins lying in wait.

However, assassins could mean a sniper on the top of a building, an explosive lobbed at his truck, a shadowy figure in a doorway waiting for the perfect shot.

He turned back to look at her, unable to help noticing how the fine silk blouse clung to her breasts and the long navy skirt hugged lush curves. Even with the frown tugging at her features she was stunning. The momentary lapse into pure male thoughts irritated him.

"My truck is parked directly out front. We're going to walk out together and you're going to get into the passenger seat as quickly as you can."

There seemed to be a touch of mutiny in her eyes, but she nodded curtly and joined him at the door. Tanner was unsure exactly what to make of the princess, but he knew his job, and that was to assure her safety. He'd get a better handle on her and the entire situation once he got her to the safety of the ranch.

He set her overnight bag just outside the door. "To the passenger side," he murmured as he wrapped her in his arms and led her out of the door. He felt her stiffen, as if she found his closeness offensive, but he didn't care. He had no idea what they might be up against, so he used his body as armor for hers as they headed toward his truck.

"I think you might be overreacting, Mr. West," she said stiffly as they moved forward together in an awkward kind of dance.

"It's your life, Princess. Would you prefer I overreact or underreact?" he asked curtly. "I'm just doing my job."

He could smell her perfume, a spicy, exotic scent that matched the smoky tones of her voice. Her body radiated warmth and the curve of her buttocks was against his legs as they moved. He felt a stir deep inside his gut, a slight rise in his pulse that both surprised and increased his irritation.

It was a relief to get her into the truck. He hurried back to the door of the office to lock it and to retrieve her bag, knowing he couldn't relax until she was safely ensconced at the ranch.

He needed to find out everything that had happened in the small country. He had to quickly learn about the coup and the escape of King Bjorn and his daughter. He needed to learn as much as he could to do his job to the best of his ability.

The fact that King Bjorn had sent his daughter to Wild West Protective Services filled him with enormous pride and a sense of responsibility that was weighty. Of course, he shouldn't be surprised that the king had sent her to them for safekeeping. After all, years ago Tanner's father, Red West, had saved the king's life.

A real, honest-to-goodness princess. She was the first royalty to come to them for protection. It was an enormous boon for the company, a huge coup for him.

He didn't have enough facts yet to know exactly what was going on, but one thing was certain; failure would put the family business and reputation on the line.

But, more than that, if what she said was true and

assassins were after her, then failure could mean the death of the pretty young woman who had placed her life in his hands.

Anna couldn't believe it. She couldn't believe her father had sent her to this man, to this place. As she'd sat on the bus that had carried her from California and into this land of dust and cows, she'd been horrified.

She couldn't believe her father had sent her to a...a cowboy for protection. Anna knew all about American cowboys, having seen a couple of Western movies. She knew they loved their horses, drank too much whiskey, ate beans out of a can and often threw their women over their shoulders like sacks of potatoes.

She watched as Tanner West strode around the front of the truck to get to the driver's door. His worn jeans hugged the long length of his legs and the cotton shirt he wore with the sleeves rolled up to the elbows exposed lean, muscled forearms.

There was something about the tall, broad-shouldered man that had instantly put her on edge. Maybe it was the calculating light in his dark green eyes, or the stern lines of his face, a face both handsome and hard. Or maybe it was because she'd known him only minutes and already he had manhandled her more than anyone else had in her life.

As he got in behind the wheel he seemed to fill the interior of the truck with a taut energy. He placed his gun between them on the seat, then started the engine and backed out of the parking space.

"This ranch of yours? Does it have amenities?" she asked.

He turned his head and cast her a quick glance, his eyes almost hidden by the low cast of the rim of his hat. "Do you mean, do we have electricity and running water? Shucks, Princess, you're in luck. We even installed indoor plumbing not long ago."

She flushed, recognizing the slight bite of sarcasm in his deep voice. "Good," she said with a forced lightness in her tone. "I wasn't sure what to expect."

"You can probably expect that things at the ranch won't be up to your usual style of life, but we'll do our best to make sure that you're comfortable for the time that you're here."

"*We?* There are other people who live on this ranch of yours?"

Despite the fact that she wasn't thrilled at the prospect of spending any length of time at a ranch, she felt herself start to relax. This would be the last place on earth any of the rebel assassins would think to look for her. They would probably check out her ritzy vacation destinations first—Miami or Vegas or New York City.

"Lots of people live on the ranch," he said in answer to her question. "It's a big spread. Besides all the men who work for us, there's my father and the rest of the family and our housekeeper, Smokey. Although right now it's just my father and Smokey. Everyone else is out on assignments."

"You have lots of bodyguards who work for you?"

"It varies at any given time."

She studied him while his focus was fixed out the window and on the road. He looked so hard, as rugged as the scenery flashing by.

There were starbursts of lines at the corners of his eyes, lines she had a feeling hadn't been created by laughter. His jaw was lean and taut and already showing the bluish black hue of a five o'clock shadow. The black hat covered much of his dark hair, but from what she'd seen of it when he'd been hatless, it was thick and had just a hint of curl.

There was nothing soft about his body, either. As he'd hovered around her on the walk to the truck, she'd felt the hardness of muscle, the heat of his body and, to her surprise and dismay, she'd found his nearness just a little bit exciting.

She thought of the bodyguards who had been assigned to her in Niflheim. They had been professionals who had adhered to a strict dress code and who had always been deferential to her wants and needs. None of them would have ever shoved her aside without apology or taken liberties by nearly smothering her with their bodies.

This man, this Tanner West, didn't look like a professional bodyguard, nor did he look like the CEO of a business. He looked like a cowboy.

"My father will expect you to assign your best bodyguard to me," she said.

"I wouldn't have it any other way," he replied in his smooth, deep voice.

Satisfied for the moment, she looked out the window and frowned at the vast expanse of nothing but plains. Occasionally a house would appear tucked between pastures and wheat fields, but the general feeling she got as she gazed out the window was one of isolation and loneliness, of civilization gone.

"This is horrible," she murmured to herself. If she'd had anything in her wallet besides a handful of credit cards, she would have run. She would have escaped this place and this man and headed for real civilization.

"Excuse me?"

She turned to look at him. "This place. It's so…so barren."

"First trip to the United States?"

"No. I travel to the States frequently. New York City is one of my favorite places in the world to visit."

"We don't have much in common with New York City," he replied.

She frowned and stared out the window once again. "I can see that. What do people do out here?"

"They live. They work. They raise families and live a simple, productive life. I'm sure it all seems quite alien to you."

She shot him a sharp glance, and met his quick

gaze. His dark green eyes were fathomless, making it impossible to discern if he'd intended to insult her or not. She decided to give him the benefit of the doubt. She suspected most cowboys were probably rough around the edges and short on social skills. He'd certainly already shown himself to be short of social skills.

Surely the man he assigned to her would be more civilized, much more understanding and respectful of her position and accustomed lifestyle.

Surely whoever was assigned to guard her wouldn't have a hard glint in his eyes or a mouth that looked as if it had never curved up in a smile. Surely he wouldn't have the subtle arrogance she sensed in Mr. Tanner West.

*I will not be intimidated by a cowboy,* she told herself. Even if that cowboy wore his jeans better than any man she'd ever seen.

"You don't have an accent," he said, breaking the uncomfortable silence.

"My nanny was American. My teachers were Americans. My father thought it important that I speak English flawlessly, without any discernible accent."

Once again silence fell between them.

He turned down a dusty two-lane road with bumps as big as the suitcases she'd been forced to leave behind at the Los Angeles airport.

Within minutes a sprawling ranch house came into view. Anna sat up straighter in the seat as he turned into the driveway. Apparently this was to be the place where she would spend her time until her father showed up or contacted her with new plans.

The house itself was neat, painted a pristine white with black shutters and trim. Colorful spring flowers bedecked the sidewalk that led up to the front door. It didn't look as bad as she'd initially expected, and for that she was grateful.

In the distance were dozens of other buildings and there were cows in a nearby pasture, their heads raised as if watching their arrival.

He parked the truck in front of the house then turned to face her. "We'll get you settled in, let you clean up, then I'll have more questions for you."

His gaze was cool, with a flinty hardness that for some reason set her pulse racing. She was accustomed to men looking at her with a certain deference and respect. She saw neither in his eyes.

"Fine. All I want right now is a place to freshen up. When will I meet the person assigned to guard me?" she asked.

"You said you wanted the best."

"I insist on it," she replied firmly.

"Then you've already met him." His eyes, those impenetrable eyes, locked with hers. "I'm the best there is. You'll be my responsibility for the duration of the time that you're here." He opened the truck door, but still held her gaze. "We'll get you settled in, I'll do a little research, then I'll go over the rules with you."

He got out of the truck, but she remained seated for a long moment. Rules? She couldn't remember the last time she'd had rules for anything. What possible rules could he attempt to impose on her?

With any luck her father would arrive soon and the threat against them would be resolved. She had a feeling she and the handsome cowboy in the tight jeans weren't going to last long together at all.

## Chapter 2

In Tanner's line of work it was important that he be a good judge of character. He had to be, to work with people as closely as he did. It had taken him all of two minutes to recognize that the princess was probably spoiled and more than a bit willful.

Niflheim was a wealthy country, and the personal wealth of King Bjorn was enormous. Tanner could be certain that Princess Anna was accustomed to a life of luxury.

Control. He had decided it was best to establish who was in control from the very beginning with the lovely princess.

He'd learned through his years in the business that

good protection wasn't possible if the agent wasn't in complete control of the potential victim. He hadn't become one of the best at this by accident.

Although officially he worked for his client in the protection business, it would only work if the client listened to him. He had to be the one in control.

Tanner retrieved her small overnight bag from the back of the pickup, then waited for her to get out of the truck. As he waited, he tried to remember everything he knew about Princess Anna Johansson of Niflheim, but nothing concrete came to mind. He was familiar with the country and with the king, but he knew nothing about the woman now in his keeping.

He'd have to do a thorough Internet search to see what he could find out about his newest assignment. He also needed to find out exactly what had happened in Niflheim and at LAX.

More than anything, it was imperative that he calculate the risk to her and establish a plan for her protection.

She got out of the truck and joined him on the sidewalk, looking none too pleased with him or the place where she found herself.

He didn't care about her happiness—he'd see to her basic creature comforts—but his main concern was to keep her alive. That's all that was important to him.

She swept past him with the imperial walk of a queen, head held high and small feet moving in purposeful strides. When she reached the front door she turned back to him, her eyes once again flashing with impatience. "Are you coming, Mr. West? I'm eager to get settled in."

He bit back a retort, joined her at the door and opened it to allow her entry. As always a sense of welcome engulfed him as he walked into the house where he'd been born and had lived most of his life.

He didn't live here in the main house anymore. Three years ago he had moved to the smaller three-bedroom house that had been the original homestead on the property when his father had bought the land years earlier.

This evening he'd move back into the main house to guard the princess 24/7.

The scent of cooking beef drifted from the kitchen. Nobody met them at the door, not that Tanner expected anyone. Smokey would be busy in the kitchen finishing up the dinner preparations and his father was probably out in the back working in the garden that had become an obsession in the past couple of years since he'd decided to semiretire from the family business.

"I'll take you to the room where you'll be staying," he said to Anna. She followed him down the long hallway that led off the entry.

When Tanner's father, Red, had married, he'd dreamed of lots of children and had built the house with a large brood in mind. The house boasted five bedrooms, four bathrooms and a dining area that could seat more than a dozen. It was perfect for a family that boasted six children.

The only people now living in the house on a regular basis were Tanner's father, Tanner's sister, Meredith, and Smokey Johnson, the cook and housekeeper.

He led Anna to what was now one of the guest rooms, a pleasant room decorated in greens and pinks with its own private bath. He set her overnight bag on the bed then turned to look at her.

She stood just inside the doorway, her gaze taking in the surroundings. She finally caught his gaze and nodded slightly, her blue eyes cool. "This will be fine for the brief time I'll be here. If you'll excuse me, I'd like to freshen up."

"You'll find everything you need in the bathroom. Dinner is in the dining room in half an hour. Don't be late." With these words he turned and left the room.

He went outside and around to the back of the house, where his father stood watering the large garden plot. Redmond West was a big man, tall with broad shoulders. He'd always been a dynamic man, but in the past couple of years he'd mellowed significantly.

A severe case of arthritis had forced Red to leave the business he loved and he'd taken to gardening as a way to pass some of the hours of the days.

Tanner quickly filled his dad in on what had transpired at the office and about their new houseguest. Red had been concerned about the king and his daugh-

ter when the reports of a coup had begun to trickle in
to the national news. All of the reports had indicated
the king had gone into hiding, but Red had feared
them dead. He was glad to hear that King Bjorn and
his daughter had escaped the country, but upset to
hear about the attack at the airport, which indicated
they were certainly not out of danger. Tanner then
went back into the house, to the study, and sat at the
desk where a computer was on and ready for his use.
Before he began his Internet search, he used his cell
phone to call two men who worked for him, arranging for them to take up guard positions at the front and
back of the house. It was just a precaution.

He used the Internet often for keeping up on the
news. The first thing he needed to do was to check any
and all stories concerning the coup in Niflheim. It
took him only minutes to learn what he needed.

The reports were sketchy and not filled with much
information other than the fact that insurgents, after
months of political unrest, had taken over the palace.
According to the news report the king and his daughter had gone into hiding.

He learned that there were two factions, a left wing
and a right wing, each attempting to gain control of
the country. Early reports were that the left-wing rad-
icals led by a man named Swensen had pulled off the
coup.

He also checked out the news about the shooting
at the airport, disappointed that the last news report

indicated that authorities had no idea what had prompted the attack or who had committed it. Because nobody had been killed, Tanner had a feeling this particular incident would fade quickly, would be shoved aside in favor of other crimes in the city.

He'd have to get more information from Anna. He needed to understand what was happening in the country and why the rebels would want her dead. She was gone from the country, so why the need for assassins?

Typing in Anna's name, he thought of the woman who was his newest assignment. Although she had full, inviting lips, there was a petulance to them that set him on edge.

As the search engine pulled up a long list of sites, he began to read the stories generated by the lovely princess.

She made the society pages frequently. Details of her jet-set lifestyle made good gossip fodder. There were pictures, as well, grainy photos of her modeling designer clothing, drinking Dom Perignon in a trendy London club and sunbathing on a yacht in the Caribbean.

He leaned back in his chair and studied one of the photos. In this particular picture she was on the dance floor in a Miami club. Her short dress exposed long, shapely legs and her head was thrown back in laughter.

Tanner knew the type. In his years in the protective services industry, he'd seen up close and personal the self-indulgent, lazy lifestyles of young men and women who had too much money and expected special treatment as their due.

After dinner he'd learn more important facts from her, facts that might help keep her alive.

He reared back in his chair, his thoughts racing. It had been almost twenty years before that his father had worked briefly for King Bjorn. The two men hadn't been in contact for years.

When Tanner had met the king at the fund-raiser in Washington he hadn't been working for the king. He couldn't see how anyone could make a connection between Wild West Protective Service and the king of Niflheim. Surely she was safe here...for the moment.

He shut off the computer and left the study, at the same time checking his wristwatch.

Life in the West household ran on a routine that was rigid yet comfortable. Dinner would be served in ten minutes and he needed to let Anna know that tardiness wasn't acceptable.

This wasn't a five-star restaurant where she could order up room service when she decided she was hungry. He didn't care what her life was like in her world. She was in his world now.

He knocked on the closed bedroom door and waited for a response. After several moments she opened the door. "Yes?" She eyed him as if he were a gnat buzzing irritably around her head.

Although she was fully dressed in the same clothes

she'd been wearing, her hair was wet and she smelled like soap, letting him know she'd used the past fifteen minutes to take a quick shower.

"Dinner will be served in five minutes. If you aren't at the table, you won't eat." He realized he sounded too abrupt, almost rude. Something about this woman set his teeth on edge. "Smokey, our cook, always has dinner ready at five-thirty," he said in an attempt to temper his abruptness.

"Then I'll be in the dining area at five-thirty." She closed the door.

Tanner sucked in a deep breath. He'd been with the woman only a little over an hour and already his irritation level had increased tenfold.

You're a professional, he reminded himself as he wandered through the great room and toward the dining room. You've worked with difficult clients before.

But none of those past clients had that silky blond hair. None of his past clients had lips that looked as if they needed to be kissed—badly.

Irritation surged up inside him and he pushed those particular thoughts aside. She was obviously spoiled, self-indulgent and demanding, negative traits certainly tempered any attraction he might feel toward her.

At five-thirty Tanner sat next to his father at the table as Smokey began to serve the evening meal. "Is the princess going to eat?" Smokey asked, his grizzly gray brows rising on his wrinkled forehead. Nobody knew Smokey's age, which he indicated was older than dirt. The old man had been the real head of the household for years.

"I have no idea what her plans are," Tanner replied as he served himself a large bowl of the beef stew. He'd told her what time dinner was served. Beyond that he had no responsibility as to whether she ate or not.

At exactly five thirty-five she entered the dining room.

"I'm sorry if I'm late," she said, although Tanner didn't think she sounded sorry at all. He wondered if perhaps her choosing to be late was a subtle form of control.

Red immediately stood and held out his hand to her. "Welcome to our home, Princess Anna. I'm Redmond West, Tanner's father and founder of Wild West Protective Services. Most folks around these parts call me Red."

"It's nice to meet you, Red. And please, just call me Anna."

"Anna it is," Red replied.

"Just Anna it has to be," Tanner said. "The last thing we want to do is let people know we have Princess Anna Johansson staying here. From now on everyone calls her Anna."

"Of course," she agreed. She smiled at Red as he held out her chair at the table.

It was the first real smile Tanner had seen on her face and it was magnificent. As her lips curved upward in the gesture all trace of petulance was gone and a warm sparkle lit her blue eyes.

The smile stirred Tanner on some base level that was distinctly uncomfortable and he looked down at his plate until she was settled in at the table.

Smokey entered from the kitchen carrying a platter of cornbread. "I see you made it in time," he said to Anna without preamble. "I hope you don't expect me to do no fancy cooking just for you. I only know one way to cook and that's plain, hearty food."

"I'm sure your cooking will be just fine," Anna said stiffly. "Besides, I don't expect to be here longer than a day, maybe two at the most. I can tolerate anything for that length of time."

Smokey snorted, slammed the platter of corn bread in front of her, then turned and disappeared back into the kitchen, which was his kingdom where he was the undisputed king.

"Don't let Smokey intimidate you," Red said. "He's all bark, but he doesn't bite hard."

"Help yourself," Tanner said, gesturing to the bowls and the stew. If she were waiting to be served, she'd have a long time to wait. "After dinner you and I need to talk."

She frowned, obviously not pleased at the prospect. "I can't imagine what we have to talk about. I've told you what happened and why I'm here. All you have to do is keep me safe until my father arrives, and I have every confidence in your ability."

"Tanner likes to cross his *t*'s and dot his *i*'s," Red said. "You might as well have a talk with him. He's a stubborn cuss and likes things done his own way." Red's voice was full of affection for his eldest son.

Anna's gaze met Tanner's and in those pretty eyes he saw a touch of calculation and more than a whisper of challenge. "All right, if you think it's absolutely necessary," she agreed.

"You know, I worked for your father many years ago," Red said as he passed her the butter.

"Really?"

"It was a long time ago, not long after your father first became king. I was in the process of building Wild West Protection Services and I'd managed to make some connections with some important people."

A wave of affection filled Tanner as he listened to his father talk. "Your father had planned a trip to New York, but he'd received information that one of his trusted bodyguards was a traitor." Red's voice was lively, his gaze fond as he eyed Anna from across the table. "King Bjorn contacted me and asked me to fly to Niflheim and accompany him on his journey. It was the biggest assignment of my career. I had to protect him not only from outside threats, but also from a potential inside threat."

"You must have been successful," she said.

Red nodded. "I managed to ferret out the traitor and keep your father safe for two weeks."

"That explains to me why my father sent me

here," she said. A frown appeared across her forehead. "Is it possible the rebels would guess that I'd be sent here?"

"I've thought about that," Tanner said. "I don't think so. As Dad said, it was years ago that he worked for your father and there has been no contact between them since then. I think you're safe here for now."

The rest of the meal consisted of good food and long, uncomfortable silences that nobody seemed inclined to fill. Tanner found himself casting surreptitious glances at her, noticing that while she ate most of the vegetables in the stew she didn't eat a lot of the beef.

He also couldn't help but notice she had the softest looking skin he'd ever seen, that her eyes were the blue of a cloudless Oklahoma sky and she had charming dimples that flashed occasionally in her cheeks.

He also saw that she had the hands of a woman who'd never worked a day in her life, soft hands with sculptured nails painted a pearly pink.

She'd made it clear she didn't want to have any sort of discussion with him, but Tanner was a thorough man and this was perhaps the biggest assignment of his career.

Whether she was under his protection for an hour or a week, he wouldn't be satisfied until he'd delved into the issues that had brought her here and had a profile of the group of men who apparently wanted her dead.

* * *

The meal had been horribly uncomfortable for
Anna. The men had been quiet and she'd been aware
that she was completely out of her element.

Throughout the tense meal, she'd found herself
casting sly glances at Tanner. She found his face in-
triguing with its lean lines and firm square jaw. There
seemed to be nothing soft about him. He was all broad
shoulders and lean muscle and cold eyes.

Every moment she spent in his company only made
her sorry she'd come to him in the first place. If circumstances were different there was no way she'd be here
in the company of a rude cook and an arrogant cowboy bodyguard. The only one who had shown her any
respect, any consideration at all, was Tanner's father.

The fear that had gripped her in those moments at
the airport in California had long passed. She felt completely safe here. She didn't feel quite as safe after dinner as she followed Tanner into the study.

She had no idea what he thought they needed to talk
about. She was beyond tired having slept little in the
past three days. The meal had only served to deepen
her exhaustion.

He closed the door behind them, then turned to face
her and gestured her toward the chair in front of the desk.
She didn't sit. As long as he was standing, she would
stand.

She looked around the room with interest, noticing
that one wall was covered with pictures. She walked

closer, recognizing photos of both Red and Tanner. There were five more pictures, four men and one woman. "Are these the agents that work for you?" she asked.

"Yes and no. They are agents, but they're also my brothers and my sister." He moved to stand next to her and pointed to each photo. "My sister is Meredith and my brothers are Zack, Clay, Joshua and Dalton."

She could smell him, that scent of sunshine and male. She also thought she could feel his body heat radiating out to envelope her.

She focused her concentration on the photos and away from him. They were a handsome family, all of them dark-haired and with the same piercing green eyes that Tanner possessed. As much as she hated to admit it, she found Tanner the most attractive of them all. "You're the eldest?" she guessed.

He nodded. "Joshua is the youngest. He's twenty-five and I'm the oldest at thirty-five. The others are scattered in between."

"And your mother?"

"Is dead," he said flatly. "Now, can we get started?" He stepped away from her and to his desk.

She wanted to tell him she was sorry about his mother. She wondered when she had died, how old had Tanner been when she'd passed away.

Anna had lost her mother when she'd been twelve and her death had left a hole in her heart and a deep abiding loneliness that had never mended.

However the expression on Tanner's face seemed to forbid any kind of sympathy, so she swallowed whatever she might have said.

She didn't sit, but remained standing and looked at the rest of the photos that decorated the wall. "These other places, they're also offices for your business?"

"Satellite offices," he replied. "Wild West Protective Services has recently opened offices in San Diego and Miami. We're hoping to open an office soon in New York." There was an undeniable ring of pride in his voice.

"How did you get started in this?"

"My father started the business years ago when he was a young man."

"And what kind of clients do you have?"

"All kinds of people from all walks of life, although much of our business comes from high-profile people—politicians, dignitaries, athletes, even a rock star or two."

It was obvious Wild West Protective Services wasn't the rinky-dink operation she'd thought when she'd first burst through the doors of the office. "Why in Cotter Creek?"

"Dad originally began in Hollywood. He was in Special Forces, and when he left the service he wasn't sure what he wanted to do, so he went to Hollywood and began working as a stuntman. It didn't take long for him to realize there was a growing need for protection for some of the stars. He began the business there, but when he decided it was time to start a family he moved the business and his new wife out here to Cotter Creek." His eyes flashed darkly. "I've answered enough of your questions. Now it's time for you to answer some of mine."

She sighed and nodded, fighting off an overwhelming weariness. "What do you need to know?"

He sat behind the desk and pulled a notepad from a drawer, then focused his gaze on her.

He was a handsome devil, she thought. His gaze held no hint of any real friendliness and she held his stare boldly and wondered what he'd look like if he smiled.

Would a smile crinkle those fine lines next to his eyes? Would a smile ease the harshness of his features into something even more handsome? She decided she didn't care. She just wanted to get this over with and retreat to the privacy of her room.

"Who are the rebels who took over the palace?" he asked.

She blinked in surprise. "I don't know…just rebels… men who obviously want my father out of power."

"Did they belong to a specific political group? Are they part of an organization of some kind?"

She leaned back in the chair. "What difference does it make? They took over the palace and now they're in control of the country." She fought a shudder as she remembered the night she'd been roused from her bed and told her life was in danger.

His mouth thinned and a muscle ticked in his jaw. "I'm not asking these questions just to be nosy. I need to know everything I can about these men. Surely you know something about the coup, something about the unrest that had to have been present before the takeover. After all, we're talking about your homeland."

There was definite censure in his voice and she sat up and straightened her shoulders defensively. "Of course I knew there was unrest."

"But perhaps you were too busy traveling, sunbathing on yachts and clubbing until dawn to pay much attention to things back home." His voice was low and smooth, but it shot a hot burst of anger through her.

"What's the matter, Mr. West—jealous? I doubt if common cowboys have many opportunities to sun on yachts or go clubbing."

His eyes glittered with a dangerous light and his lips curved upward in a smile that wasn't particularly pleasant. "Trust me, Princess. I might be a cowboy, but there's nothing common about me."

She sighed impatiently. "Are you always this rude to clients?" She didn't wait for him to reply, but instead stood. "If all you intend to do is bait me, then I think I'll call it a night."

"Please." The muscle in his jaw ticked faster. "I apologize. This is important."

She hesitated, torn between wanting to run to her room and hide and the desire to show him she could take whatever he wanted to dish out. The latter won and she returned to the chair.

He gave a deep sigh and raked a hand through his hair. "Let me explain something to you," he said once she was seated. "One of the first things I do is create a profile on whomever is after my client. From the profile I try to figure out what might be the potential threat."

Anna sighed wearily. "I just think this is all unnecessary. I'm sure my father will be here in a day or so and there's no possible way the rebels could know I'm here. I wasn't even sure I'd come here when I left California. I'm sure there's no danger for me here."

"We can't know that for sure," he countered. "We can't know that unless I can identify the rebel forces, find out what kind of communication they have, what kind of technology they possess."

Again he surprised her. "I didn't know bodyguards concerned themselves with these kinds of things," she said slowly.

"Maybe others don't, but Wild West Protective Services is one of the best. Why do you think your father sent you here?"

"To punish me," she muttered under her breath.

He leaned forward in his chair, ignoring her reply. "I'll ask you again—what can you tell me about the rebel forces that took over the palace in Niflheim?"

She frowned thoughtfully, reluctantly admitting to herself that she hadn't paid much attention to such things. But, she certainly didn't intend to admit it out loud to him.

"The unrest in Niflheim wasn't something new, but in the past couple of months it has become much more intense. There were some people who believed it was time for the monarchy to fall and a new kind of government to take its place. The rebels who took over the palace want a parliamentary kind of government."

"And what does your father think?"

"I don't know for sure. My father doesn't confide in me about such matters." She could tell by his narrowed eyes that her answer didn't please him.

"According to the news reports the country is now in the hands of these rebels. They have what they want. Why would they want you and your father dead?"

"I don't know for sure. Maybe they're afraid my father will rally his supporters and attempt to reclaim the country. My father is not a man without loyal supporters. Maybe they're afraid that they'll never really have control unless we're in a position to never return."

He leaned forward, his gaze hard and focused. "Are these rebels organized? Is there a leader of their forces? Did you ever hear your father mention the names of these men?" The questions hit her like bullets.

"No…I don't know." Why hadn't she paid more attention to what was happening around her in Niflheim? "There was a group my father was concerned about, a radical group...but I can't remember their name." Exhaustion overwhelmed her and once again she stood. "I'm tired. I can't think anymore. We'll finish this tomorrow when I've rested."

"I certainly don't want to push you too hard," he said, an edge of coolness to his voice.

"You don't like me very much, do you?" she asked.

His gaze shifted away from her. "It doesn't matter whether I like you or not," he replied.

"If it's any consolation to you, I don't like you very much, either." She exited the office, breathing easier the minute she was out of his presence.

One thing was certain. He'd been right when he'd said that he wasn't a common cowboy. Tanner West was far more than that. It had been obvious from the story told by the photos on the wall in the office that Wild West Protective Services wasn't just a small family operation. It had also been obvious by the questions Tanner had wanted answered that he possessed a keen intelligence.

Smart and handsome, and something about him put her on edge, made her feel both vulnerable and defensive. She entered the bedroom where she would be staying and walked to the window.

Outside the sun had dipped below the horizon and darkness had begun to claim the sky. From this vantage point she could see nothing but pasture for as far as the eye could see.

A well of loneliness filled her. It wasn't a new emotion, but it had never been as intense as it was at this moment. She was stuck in a place she didn't want to be with an arrogant, hateful man who obviously didn't like her. She didn't want to be here but was powerless to go anywhere else.

She walked over to the bed and sat on the edge, pulling her overnight bag closer. She felt as if she'd been thrust into a horrid nightmare. As if the coup hadn't been bad enough, she now had to contend with Tanner West until her father arrived.

She opened the bag and withdrew the velvet pouch inside. Her fingers trembled slightly as she opened the pouch and withdrew the jeweled crown. It wasn't a large crown, but it held an array of flawless rubies, emeralds and diamonds.

Placing it on the top of her head, she leaned back against the pillows on the bed. She was Princess Anna Johansson of Niflheim and she wasn't about to let some arrogant cowboy bodyguard boss her around.

She pulled the crown from her head, once again filled with an overwhelming sense of loneliness. She hoped her father came for her soon and she could get back to her life of friends and parties and pleasures, a lifestyle that had always managed to keep that aching loneliness at bay.

# Chapter 3

Tanner sat at the kitchen table reading through the information he'd printed off the Internet the night before. He'd worked long past midnight, searching obscure sites and trying to find whatever he could about Niflheim and the social unrest that had plagued the country.

He'd discovered that John Swenson, the leader of the left faction, had control of the palace but did not have control of the countryside and nobody seemed willing to guess who would eventually win total control.

He also tried to find out where King Bjorn was now, but he was unsuccessful. It was as if the king had dropped off the face of the earth following the shooting at LAX.

It was now just after ten. Breakfast had come and gone hours ago and still Anna hadn't put in an appearance. Not that he was surprised. She was probably accustomed to sleeping late, breakfasting in bed, personal servants and social assistants.

While she slept the day away, he'd been busy. He'd gone to his own place and packed a bag, then had moved into the room next to hers. For the duration of her stay here, he'd be here, as well. He'd also arranged for four trusted ranch hands to work eight-hour shifts as guards on the house, then be replaced by new, fresh men.

The rest of the morning he'd spent on the computer printing off anything and everything he'd missed the night before that pertained to the small Scandinavian Island of Niflheim and the shoot-out at LAX.

It would have been nice if Anna had been able to answer more of his questions the night before. But, he supposed it had been too much to expect that the jetsetting princess would have any clue about what might have been going on in her own country. It was hard to be in touch with the people's needs when you were partying until dawn and shopping until you dropped.

"You want anything before I head to the laundry room?" Smokey asked from behind Tanner.

"No thanks, I'm fine," he replied.

"You suppose that woman will ever make it to a meal on time?"

Tanner turned in his chair and grinned at Smokey. "Who knows what that woman is going to do?"

"She's a pretty little thing even if she isn't worth a hill of beans," Smokey replied as he washed a coffee cup in the sink, then placed it in the dish drainer to dry.

"Is this where I come to be served breakfast?" Anna appeared in the kitchen doorway.

Smokey snorted. "I cook breakfast once a day, serve it at dawn. If you snooze, you lose. I ain't going to start changing my ways just because there's a princess in the house." With another snort, Smokey disappeared out the back door.

"My goodness, this house is full of disagreeable men," she said as she came into the kitchen and sat on the chair across from Tanner.

Tanner bit back the sharp reply that leaped to his tongue. He didn't want to start the day with a battle. "Smokey really isn't so disagreeable. I told you before, we have a routine in the house, a routine that was initially set up the year my mother died and Smokey wound up as cook and housekeeper. With six kids there had to be routines and rules. One of the cardinal rules of the house is if you aren't at the table when a meal is served, then you don't eat."

"All right, so breakfast is at dawn. What time is dawn?"

He eyed her narrowly, unsure if she was being sarcastic or not. She appeared to be quite serious. "Around six. Would you like a cup of coffee?"

She nodded and he got up from the table and went to a nearby cabinet to retrieve a mug. "If you want breakfast, I could probably rustle you up something," he offered grudgingly.

"Heavens, no. I wouldn't want to put anyone out. Coffee is fine."

"I guess you slept well," he said.

"Like a log. I hadn't slept much since the scene at the airport. I just got a few catnaps on the bus ride here. I was really exhausted. How old were you when your mother died?"

He blinked at the quick change in topic, then hesitated, unsure why she felt compelled to know this personal history of his. "Ten," he finally answered, realizing it might build some trust between them. "Cream or sugar?"

"No, black is fine."

He set the cup in front of her, then returned to his chair. "I was twelve when I lost my mother," she said. "I think it was the worst thing that's ever happened to me."

She took a sip of the coffee, eyeing him over the rim of the cup. "She had breast cancer and it wasn't caught soon enough. She went far too quickly. What about your mother? How did she die?"

"She was murdered."

Anna gasped and placed a hand on his forearm. "I'm so sorry," she exclaimed, her blue eyes radiating a compassion that surprised him. "That must have been horrible for you...for all of you."

Her hand felt dainty and warm on his bare skin. He moved his arm from beneath her hand, finding her touch far too appealing. "It was a long time ago," he said.

He picked up one of the pieces of paper in front of him and pretended to study it as she drank her coffee and stared out the window as if lost in her own thoughts.

She'd surprised him with that burst of sympathy that seemed at odds with the woman she'd shown herself to be in the short time he'd known her.

He stared at the paper and thought about his mother. It had been twenty-five years ago that his mother had been murdered on her way home from town. Twenty-five years ago and still Tanner felt the rip in his heart.

The night that her body had been found sprawled next to her car had been the only time Tanner had ever seen his father weep. That night had changed Tanner's life forever.

"The mist," Anna said suddenly, looking at him as if she'd surprised herself.

"Pardon me?"

She frowned and stared down into her coffee mug. "In Scandinavian mythology before Creation there were two places. Muspellsheim—"

"The land of fire," he said. Her gaze shot back at him and surprise once again lit her eyes. She was probably shocked that a stupid cowpoke would know such a thing. In truth yesterday he wouldn't have known about the myth, but his reading that morning had enlightened him.

"That's right. Muspellsheim was the land of fire and Niflheim was the land of ice and mist."

"Is there a reason for you mentioning this?" he asked, wondering where she was going. "Or is it that you just think I need a mythology lesson?"

"Yes…I mean no. The radical group—they call themselves something of the mist. Warriors of the Mist or Men of the Mist, or something like that. It just popped into my head." She looked inordinately pleased with herself.

"Good," Tanner said. "Maybe with that much information I can find out more about them. I already tried to find what I could on John Swenson, who apparently leads the rebels. But I couldn't find any information on him or his group."

"Did you find out anything about my father? Where he is now? If he's all right?"

He shook his head, wishing he had news for her. "Nothing. We can only assume that he's been taken into some sort of protective custody and will contact us when he can.

"Betrayed? What do you mean?" She wrapped her slender fingers around the coffee mug as if she needed to hang on to something concrete to hear what he had to say.

"There's no way assassins could have been waiting for you at the airport without knowing specifically what flight you and your father were on. They'd have to have known the time of your arrival and where you'd exit the airport, to lie in wait for you."

Her eyes grew wider with each word he spoke. "I hadn't thought about that," she said in a low, troubled voice.

"Who knew your flight information besides you and your father?"

"I don't know." She took a sip of the coffee, that charming frown back between her brows. "I don't know how the arrangements were made."

How could a twenty-five-year-old woman be so clueless, so uninformed about the forces that were driving her life? He couldn't imagine not being in control of his own destiny.

She raised her chin. "I can't imagine that anyone would betray us. I can't imagine anyone who was close enough to us could be capable of doing something like that."

"There's no other explanation for those men to have been at the airport at the right time, at the right exit."

He sighed and raked a hand through his hair impatiently. "Okay, then I'll see what I can dig up on this group of the mist or whatever."

"While you're doing that, I have some things to take care of myself."

Tanner eyed her warily. "Like what?"

"Hopefully there is a car that will be at my disposal while I'm here. If not, I can call a car service."

A car service in Cotter Creek? She'd have as much luck looking for an ocean in Oklahoma. The princess had no idea how normal people lived, he thought.

"One way or another I simply must go into town," she continued. "As you can see, I'm wearing the same clothes I've worn since my arrival in Los Angeles. I definitely need to do some shopping and I thought perhaps I'd get lunch while I was out."

Any modicum of amusement at her ignorance of a small town disappeared as he stared at her, for a moment at a complete loss for words.

"Are you insane?" he finally managed to exclaim.

She sat back in the chair, obviously offended. "Of course I'm not insane."

"Well, you aren't going anywhere." He stood. The abrupt motion sent his chair skittering backward along the wooden floor. "Especially not alone. What do you think this is? Some sort of vacation?"

She stood, as well, her blue eyes flashing with anger. "Of course not, but I think you're forgetting something, Mr. West. I'm your client, not your prisoner, and you can't stop me from going wherever I want." There was an edge of haughtiness in her voice coupled with more than a measure of stubborn resolve.

She turned to leave the room, but in three long strides he caught her by the arm, whirled her around and pulled her up against him.

"Listen, lady, I've worked my ass off for the last fifteen years to give this company the reputation of one that doesn't make mistakes. I'm not about to let you be my first mistake. If you're my client, then start acting like it instead of acting like a spoiled brat."

She gasped and her face paled. "Let go of me. How dare you speak to me that way." Her voice trembled and he released her, fully expecting her to run and lock herself in her room or some other such dramatic nonsense. He half expected her to yell, "Off with his head!"

Instead she straightened her shoulders and stood her ground. "I need some clothes and some personal items. If you don't want me to go to town by myself, then you take me or you send somebody to get the things I need." Her voice was deceptively calm.

The burst of anger that had exploded between them had astonished Tanner and he took a moment to intake a deep breath and steady himself.

The small overnight bag she'd brought with her hadn't been big enough to carry more than a few personal toiletry items. He reluctantly had to admit that she probably needed some clothes, especially if she was going to be on the ranch for any length of time. His sister Meredith's clothes wouldn't work, as Meredith was considerably taller that Anna.

"Be ready in fifteen minutes and I'll drive you into town to get what you need," he said against his better judgment. At least if he took her, he could control where she went and who got next to her.

"I'll be ready." She turned and started to leave the kitchen, but paused and turned back to face him. "And don't think for one minute you're going to throw me over your shoulder." She whirled around once again and stomped off in the direction of her bedroom.

Tanner stared after her, wondering what in the hell that meant. He took another deep breath and sank into a chair at the kitchen table once again. He couldn't remember the last time a woman had so riled him. And that anger had ignited so quickly.

What was it about her that had managed to push him over the edge of control? Tanner rarely lost his temper, but in the space of a few minutes she'd managed to make him lose all control.

Maybe it was the fact that she'd slept so late, or that she'd entered the kitchen apparently expecting somebody to serve her breakfast. Maybe it was the highfalutin tone in her voice.

It wasn't just the anger that had exploded so fast between them that had surprised him. He'd been shocked by the instantaneous streak of desire that had gripped him as he'd yanked her up tight against him.

Somewhere in the back of his mind, even though he'd been irritated with her, he'd registered the soft press of her breasts against his chest. His mind had heeded her scent, that provocative spicy fragrance that had been in his head since the moment she'd first walked into his office.

He didn't particularly like her. He certainly saw

nothing in her to respect or admire. But apparently that didn't matter to his body, for it had responded to her nearness with an intensity that had shocked him.

On some base perverse level he wanted her. And that was absolutely unacceptable. One of the worst things he could do as a bodyguard was get personally involved with a client.

Part of the problem was that Tanner couldn't remember the last time he'd been so attracted to a woman. For the last couple of years his work had consumed him. When this assignment was over, maybe he'd take a little time to attend to his personal life.

In the meantime, if what Anna believed was correct, then her father should show up here any day, any minute, for that matter, and that was just fine with Tanner.

The sooner he got rid of her, the better.

Anna stood in the bedroom, heart pounding in an unsteady rhythm. Tanner West was the most arrogant, aggravating and bossy man she'd ever met.

She grabbed her hairbrush from the dresser and dragged it through her hair, her thoughts still focused on Tanner and the scene they'd just had.

With a single glance of those wicked green eyes of his he could manage to make her feel stupid. And she wasn't stupid. Still, it wasn't the spat they'd just had that had shaken her.

What made her feel slightly unsteady, a little bit

breathless, was that moment when he'd yanked her up against him and that stern mouth of his had been mere inches from hers. She'd had an overwhelming impulse to kiss him, to see if those lips of his were softer than they looked. She'd wanted his eyes to flame with something other than cold disdain.

That impulse to kiss him irritated her more than his bossiness, more than the fact that he could make her feel stupid.

"Ouch," she muttered as she pulled her hair. She set the brush down and applied a touch of pink lipstick, dabbed some powder on her nose.

She had a feeling Tanner West was a man who was accustomed to people jumping when he spoke. Well, she didn't jump for any man, especially not a dusty cowboy.

She refused to allow Tanner to ruin her day with his ill temper. She was looking forward to going into town, eager to buy some clothing and burn the ones she'd been wearing for too long. At least the little trip would be something to do, a way to pass a couple of hours.

Aware that Tanner had said to be ready in fifteen minutes and that he was a man who obviously worshiped the clock, she left her room and went in search of him. She found him in the kitchen talking to his father.

"Good morning, Anna." Red offered her a warm smile. How did such a nice man get a son like Tanner? she wondered.

"Good morning, Mr. West," she replied.

"Please, I told you yesterday at dinner to call me Red."

"Then Red it is." She smiled at him. He was really quite nice. He was easy to see where Tanner got his height and broad shoulders for his father has the same attributes. Unlike Tanner, Red's eyes were blue, but the shape of their faces was the same, with the strength of a firm jaw and chiseled features.

"You might want to keep an eye on the sky," Red said. "The weatherman is calling for some strong storms moving in sometime this afternoon."

"Then we'd better get started," Tanner said, his voice brusque.

"We'll see you later, Red," she said, then hurried to follow Tanner's long strides as he walked toward the door.

Minutes later she was back in the dusty black pickup with Tanner behind the wheel. "Do you have bad storms here?" she asked once they were on their way.

"Sometimes."

"I've never liked storms," she said more to herself than to him. It had been storming the night her mother had died. She remembered that night as if it had happened yesterday. The storm had raged at the windows while inside her mother had finally given up her fight with the illness that had tormented her. Since that night rainstorms had always brought with them a sense of dread and loss for Anna.

"Before we get into town I want to go over the rules with you," he said.

She shoved her painful thoughts away and raised an eyebrow. "There are rules for going into town?"

He cast her a quick glance beneath the rim of his hat. "There are rules for everything you do while you're under my protection."

She released an audible sigh. "I'm not accustomed to rules."

"Get accustomed."

"Fine, tell me your rules, then I'll tell you some rules of my own." She intended to try to be as pleasant as possible for the duration of having to suffer his company.

"I'm not thrilled to be making this trip."

"Yes, I have that impression."

"I'll take you to a store where you should be able to get everything you need, but rule number one is that you don't leave my side…not for an instant. If anyone asks, and they probably will, your name is Anne Jones and you're a friend of mine from New York."

"Won't that make people suspicious?"

"What do you mean?" he asked.

"The fact that you have a friend."

A muscle ticked in his jaw, letting her know she'd scored a small point. "I was on assignment in New York last month," he said. "If anyone asks. That's when we met each other. The second rule is that once we're out in public you understand that you could be at risk. If I ask you to do anything, you comply immediately. You don't hesitate and you don't ask questions, you just do what I tell you to do."

She slid him a sideways glance. "You like that, don't you?"

"What?"

"You like having people who ask how high when you tell them to jump."

"Don't be ridiculous. I'm just doing my job."

"Is that it?"

"For now."

"Okay, now here are my rules." She sat up straighter in the seat. "When we're out in public you treat me with respect and you stop looking at me like I'm stupid, because I'm not."

"I never said you were stupid," he countered. "Is that it?"

"No, I have one more." She saw his fingers tighten around the steering wheel. "You have to get me something to eat while we're out. I missed breakfast and I have a feeling we won't make lunch and that means that cranky old cook of yours won't feed me again until dinnertime."

A whisper of a smile curved his lips, softening his features and sending an unexpected curl of heat through her stomach. "If Smokey heard you call him a 'cranky old cook' he'd tie you to Dante's horns."

"Who's Dante?"

"The biggest, meanest bull in the Midwest."

She noticed his hands had relaxed on the steering wheel. She turned her attention out the passenger window, wondering about that momentary surge of heat that had swept through her when he'd smiled.

Hunger, she decided. That had been a hunger pang, nothing more. She looked at him once again. "Smokey…how did he come to work for your family?"

"Smokey worked as my father's foreman. He took care of things on the ranch while Dad worked Wild West Protective Services," Tanner told her, then continued. "Two months before my mother's murder Smokey was thrown from a horse and trampled nearly to death." He shook his head. "My father always refers to that summer as the black summer."

"It must have been terrible," she said softly.

He gave a curt nod. "Anyway, with Mom's death and with Smokey no longer able to take care of the ranch work, Dad brought him into the house to help out. Smokey held us all together while we were growing up." His affection for the old man was obvious in his voice.

"Has he always been so…so…" She fought to find a word to describe Smokey.

"Yes," he replied. "Smokey has always been gruff and outspoken. But he also has a knack for organization, runs the house like a well-oiled machine and has a heart of gold."

She digested this information, unsure that she believed the crabby old man had a heart at all. "Your brothers and sister, do they all work for the agency?"

"All of them except Joshua. He left about a year ago and moved to New York City."

"Really? What does he do there?" She had a feeling she'd like the urban Joshua far better than she liked Tanner.

"He's a stockbroker." A wrinkle furrowed his brow.

"Where is everyone else?" she asked, curious about him and his family. As an only child Anna had always wondered what it would be like to have siblings.

The wrinkle disappeared from his forehead. "Right now we're all pretty well scattered to the wind. Zack is closest. He's on assignment in Oklahoma City. Clay is in New Orleans. Dalton is in Las Vegas and Meredith is down in Texas."

"You're close to all of them?"

He shot her a quick glance. "I'd die for any one of them."

A wave of longing stuck her as the familiar loneliness welled up inside her. She stuffed it down, refusing to allow it to take hold of her. "Tell me more about your family. What are they like? Are your brothers as mean and bossy as you are?"

Those green eyes splashed her with a look of cool mock indignation. "I'm not mean, except with people who force me to be."

She ignored his little dig. "Are your brothers and your sister as good as you are at this protection stuff?"

"No, but eventually they will be. I've answered enough of your questions. You talk too much."

"Just practicing a little civility, but I'm sure that's alien to you." She fell silent as she saw the small town of Cotter Creek in the distance.

She hadn't explored the town when she'd first arrived. She'd gotten off the bus and had gone directly to the offices of Wild West Protective Services.

As Tanner turned down what appeared to be the main street, she looked around with interest. They passed a post office, a bank and a grocery store.

The buildings looked ancient and were covered with the dust that seemed to be everywhere. Still, there was a certain charm in the stately old structures. Pots of bright-colored flowers decorated the front of many of the stores and awnings shielded the windows from the midday sun.

Tanner pulled up in front of a store with a pink awning and the words Betty's Boutique on the plate-glass window. A pleasant relief swept through her as she realized within minutes she would have new clothes to replace the ones she'd had on since the shooting at the airport in California.

Tanner cut the engine, unbuckled his seat belt and turned to look at her. "Okay, we go in, get what you need, then get out."

"Wait…I have a problem," she said as a sudden thought struck her.

"What?"

"I don't have any money. I spent my cash on the bus

ticket from California. I have a wallet full of credit cards but I have a feeling that's the last thing you'd want me to use."

"A credit card purchase would be an easy trail for somebody to follow," he said. "Don't worry about it. Get what you need and I'll charge it to our account."

"I'll pay you back," she assured him. "As soon as my father arrives, I'll see that you're paid back for any expense you have incurred."

"I'm not worried about it."

"I am. I don't want to owe you anything."

He nodded and together they got out of the truck.

She certainly hadn't expected designer fashions or a vast selection, but nothing had quite prepared her for Betty's Boutique.

The center of the store held racks that were filled with sturdy jeans and cotton shirts in all sizes. At the left of the store was a single rack of dresses, dresses that Anna could tell at a glance were like nothing she'd ever worn before.

"Morning, Tanner," a chirpy little voice called from the back of the store. The voice belonged to a plump, gray-haired woman who hurried toward them. "Don't see you in here too often." She gazed with open curiosity at Anna. "And who might this be?"

"Anne, this is Betty. She owns the store. Betty, this is Anne, she's a friend of mine from back east," Tanner said.

"I knew she wasn't from around here, not with

them fancy shoes." She pointed to Anna's dainty navy sling-back shoes.

"Actually, I'm from New York City," Anna said. "And it's nice to meet you, Betty."

Betty smiled at Anna, a sly smile. "Now I see why Tanner doesn't dally with any of the local women."

Anna sensed Tanner stiffening beside her. With impish mischief she smiled up at him and grabbed his arm. "He might not dally with the local women, but trust me, he dallies just fine. Don't you, darling?"

Tanner's arm was so rigid she felt that if she moved it just a little it would snap in two. A quick glance up at him let her know he was angry and eventually she'd pay, but at the moment she didn't care.

Betty released a high-pitched laugh, then winked at Anna. "I knew he probably had some pretty woman stashed somewhere. The rest of those West boys have always liked the women. Now, what can I do for you folks today?"

"I'm in need of some new clothing," Anna said as she released Tanner's arm.

"Ranch clothes," he said. Tanner placed an arm around her shoulder and smiled down at her, his eyes gleaming with what couldn't be mistaken for anything but payback. "My sweet Anne arrived with suitcases full of fancy designer things, but nothing strictly functional for mucking out stables and helping out around the place."

In that instant Anna saw her dreams of a couple of

sweet little dresses fly right out the window. She was unsure what "ranch clothes" were, but was certain she probably wouldn't like them.

"And boots," he added. "She definitely needs a pair of good, sturdy boots."

Half an hour later Anna stood in front of the counter and watched Betty ring up the purchases: three pairs of jeans, several T-shirts and short sleeved cotton shirts, and a pair of boots.

She'd picked out the boots herself, insisting on a red pair. Tanner and Betty had chosen the rest of the items. They'd even picked out a hat for her, a brown cowboy hat that she thought looked ridiculous on her head.

She had managed to snag two bras without a hint of lace on either one of them and several pairs of pant-ies…no-nonsense white cotton. It had amused her that Tanner had looked distinctly uncomfortable as she'd made the underwear selection.

He might be the best bodyguard in the world, but he was obviously a man not comfortable with all things feminine and somehow that weakness made him less intimidating and more human.

They were just about to leave the store when he turned to her, a frown once again riding the center of his forehead. "We didn't get you nightclothes," he said. "Don't you need a gown or a pair of pajamas or some-thing?"

With the knowledge of his discomfort in mind, she

smiled sweetly. "Oh no, that's not necessary. I always sleep in the nude." To her immense satisfaction his face blanched then filled with color as the muscle in his jaw ticked overtime.

# Chapter 4

Tanner could have lived a long time without knowing that the princess slept in the nude. The minute the words left her mouth he'd been cursed with a vision that had sent his pulse rocketing and had dried every ounce of moisture from his mouth.

Shopping with her had been difficult enough. It had been obvious by the expression on her face that she hadn't been thrilled about the sturdy jeans and no-nonsense shirts he and Betty had chosen for her, although she proclaimed to adore the boots she'd picked out, a scarlet red pair embossed with flowers.

It had been particularly uncomfortable to watch her paw through the panties and bras, commenting that they were all so simple and plain. He had a feeling even simple and plain would look sexy on her.

He shifted the bag of her new clothes from one hand to the other, trying to think about something else.

She seemed to be holding no grudge after their spat in the kitchen earlier this morning. That surprised him. He'd thought she would be the type to pout and hold a grudge long after the fact.

He now stood outside the shop, waiting for Anna. He shifted from foot to foot, fighting a wave of impatience. Not all of the new purchases were in the bag. She'd insisted that she change into some of her new clothes before leaving the store.

Knowing that they'd been alone in the store with Betty, he'd decided to step outside to wait for her. He knew Betty kept the back door of the shop locked so the only way for anyone to get inside was through him, which wasn't going to happen unless he knew the person trying to enter posed no threat.

As he waited for her, he tried to shove the image of a naked Anna from his head and instead focus on his surroundings.

He knew this town and most of the people in it. He saw no strangers walking the streets, no reason to be concerned or alarmed for Anna's safety.

There seemed to be little chance that the assassins would guess that Anna would take a bus to a small Oklahoma town. He thought she was probably safe for the moment, but that didn't mean he intended to relax his vigil.

The gun tucked into the waistband of his jeans and hidden by the tails of his untucked shirt was a familiar companion, as was the knife strapped to his shin. He knew how to use both quite effectively and hoped he wouldn't have to while Anna was in his care.

"I look positively ridiculous."

He whirled around to see her standing in the doorway of the shop. Again his mouth went unaccountably dry and his pulse rate accelerated. The jeans fit her like a second skin, showing off her slender waist and clinging to her long legs.

The scarlet-red T-shirt matched her boots and the color enhanced her creamy complexion and blond hair. The shirt also pulled taut across her full breasts.

The cowboy hat sat on the very back of her head, looking as if it would slide off and to the ground, if she moved her head at all.

She didn't look ridiculous. She looked like a model that had stepped off the cover of a cowboy calendar. All she needed was a big horse and a lasso and she'd be every cowpoke's fantasy.

"You look fine. You now look like you belong in Cotter Creek," he replied, his voice sounding deeper than usual to his own ears.

"Now you're really scaring me," she said dryly.

He stepped closer to her and grabbed her hat,

adjusting it more on the crown on her head. "There. That's the way to wear a cowboy hat."

"Thanks, pardner," she drawled, her breath warm and sweet on his face. For a brief moment they remained mere inches from each other. Her scent surrounded him and he had the craziest impulse to press his mouth to hers. Her lips parted, as if in open invitation.

He jumped back from her, uncomfortable by their nearness and the crazy direction of his thoughts. What the hell was he thinking? "Where's your other things?" he asked, aware that she'd come out of the store empty-handed.

She waved her hands in dismissal. "I told Betty to throw them away. I certainly don't ever want to see that blouse and skirt again."

"She'll probably iron them up and hang them on a rack for resale. Not that people here have much use for designer clothes."

"If she can sell them, that's fine with me. I certainly don't want them anymore."

"Let's get these things in the truck."

"Lunch. You promised," she reminded him.

"I haven't forgotten," he replied. He really didn't like the idea of making her any more visible in the town. The less people who knew she was out at the ranch, the better.

But there were few secrets in Cotter Creek and Betty would probably already be buzzing to somebody about Tanner West's fancy big-city girlfriend. Trying to keep a secret was almost as impossible as having one in this small town.

It was easier to take her to lunch and to let people think she was a girlfriend visiting from out of town. Let people think he had nothing to hide. Besides, the lunch crowd was usually small and they should be able to eat and get out in a short period of time.

"We'll go to the café, but if I see somebody I don't recognize inside, we're going to head right back to the ranch," he explained as he stored her purchases inside the cab of his pickup.

She eyed him through narrowed eyelids. "You wouldn't pretend to see a stranger just to screw up lunch for me, would you?"

At first he assumed she was just giving him a hard time, but as he held her gaze he saw that she was serious. It surprised him, that she thought he would do something like that.

"Anna, you might not like me. You might think I'm bossy and controlling, but I wouldn't lie to you just to steal a little pleasure from you. Now, let's go get some lunch."

To his vast relief, she said nothing, but merely nodded, those big blue eyes of hers studying him as he led her toward the Sunny Side Up Café.

"The dining choices are limited here in Cotter Creek," he said as they crossed the street.

"Well, there's a surprise," she said, again that edge of dry humor in her tone.

He ignored her quip. "There's the café and a pizza place about four miles up the road just off the highway."

"Right now I'm so hungry you could just tie me up to Dante and I'd eat him," she said, and grinned up at him.

That grin filled her face with warm invitation and sparked her eyes and, for just a moment, she wasn't a princess with an attitude. She wasn't spoiled, lazy and demanding. She was just a very pretty young woman whose smile warmed him from the inside out.

Again he had a flash of a mental image of her naked in bed, her body sleep-warmed and her blond hair in tousled disarray.

She'd thrown him off balance almost from the get-go this morning, first irritating him to distraction with their argument, then flashing tantalizing glimpses of her sense of humor on the drive into town.

"Don't get too comfortable over lunch," he said gruffly. "I've got a lot of things to do when we get back to the ranch."

He was eager to get back to the computer. With the tidbit of information she'd told him earlier, that the rebels name had something to do with mist, he was hoping he could find something that would give him a handle on who he was dealing with.

While he worked on the computer she could surely

find something to do to entertain herself. He could use a little distance from her, at least until the thought of her naked body completely left his brain.

"Not much of a lunch crowd, is there?" she murmured as they walked into the Sunny Side Up. Two old-timers sat at the long counter that stretched along one wall and three middle-aged women sat at a table near the front of the café.

They were all familiar faces and Tanner felt himself relax a bit as he recognized the place held no obvious danger for a princess. He swept his hat off his head and she did the same.

"They do a good breakfast and dinner business, but at lunchtime most folks are too busy to have lunch out," he explained.

"Busy doing what?" she asked.

"Working. That's what most people do out here." He led her toward a table in the rear, where he could sit with his back to the wall and face the doorway.

He walked just behind her, trying not to notice how the tight jeans molded to her shapely backside. She sat across from him and immediately picked up one of the worn menus on the table.

"The rest rooms are down this hallway," he said, gesturing to the hallway next to their table. "Beyond the rest rooms is a back door." He spoke in a low voice. "If there's any problems and I tell you to run, you run out the back door and to the sheriff's office three doors down."

"I still don't think I'm in any danger here. Nobody in their right mind would look for me in a place like Cotter Creek."

That highbrow tone was back in her voice and he did his best to ignore it. "You're probably right, but I'm not willing to let down my guard until your father arrives and I know you're in good hands," he replied. "The reputation of my company rests on me keeping you safe."

"It's possible by the time we get back to the ranch he will have arrived. Then I won't need all the clothes and things you bought for me." She sounded pleased at this thought.

He shrugged and opened his menu. "I can always take them back." He'd like to take them all back right now and get bigger sizes for her.

As she studied the menu, Tanner scanned the interior of the café once again, then looked at his menu.

"Hey, Tanner."

He looked up to see Shelia Burnwell waving to him from the doorway. He nodded a hello.

"When are you going to get your old man to sell?" she asked.

"Won't happen in this lifetime."

She moved in displeasure and took a seat on the opposite side of the café.

"Who's that?" Anna asked curiously.

"A local Realtor. She's had her eye on our place for some time."

Their conversation was interrupted by the appearance of their waitress.

When the waitress left, Anna leaned back in the chair, looking pleased as punch to be someplace where someone worked.

"Tell me something, Tanner. Why don't you dally with any of the local women?" she asked, a mischievous twinkle in her eyes. "Are you gay?"

"Of course not," he exclaimed. The woman was impossible. She was not only spoiled, but far too outspoken for his taste. Most people didn't talk about their sexuality so openly.

"You know, it's nothing to be ashamed of if you are," she continued. She pulled a paper napkin from the container in the center of the table and spread it over her lap. "I know lots of gay men and I also know that men who are conflicted about it sometimes come off as overly macho and controlling."

"I'm not gay," he repeated tersely as he felt his irritation with her rising once again. "I just don't date much. I don't have time."

"Don't you ever want to get married? Have some children?"

"Sure, eventually that's what I want. When I think the time is right." In fact, over the course of the past year the desire had become more intense. He did want a family of his own, but only when he found the perfect woman who would accept his commitment to his job.

"I've been focused on building up the business since the time I was twenty years old," he explained. "That's taken up all my time and energy."

"You have to make time to have fun. It's what makes you a healthy, balanced person. You know what they say about all work and no play."

"Yeah. I wonder what they say about all play and no work," he said pointedly. The last thing he needed or wanted was a lecture about working from a woman who'd probably never done an honest day's work in her life.

Her delicate eyebrows pulled together as she frowned. "It's impossible to have any kind of a reasonable conversation with you, so I'm not even going to try anymore. You're an impossible man, Tanner West, and if I wasn't so hungry, I'd get up and leave right now."

At that moment the waitress appeared with their orders. Tanner tried to concentrate on his food and not on her. He hoped she was right. He hoped they returned to the ranch and her father was there waiting for her. She'd been in Tanner's care less than twenty-four hours and for some reason was burrowing into his skin like an irritating tick.

For the first time in his life he couldn't wait for an assignment to be over.

Respect had been Anna's birthright and something she'd never thought about much before. She'd commanded it without doing a thing, by merely being born into royalty. For most of her life people had fawned over her, talked to her with homage.

However, it was obvious that Tanner didn't respect her and it surprised her that she was bothered by it. He might be the CEO of a big company, but he was also obviously uncivilized and socially unpolished.

What did she care if some hard-ass cowboy bodyguard didn't respect her? What difference did it make to her whether he liked her or not? He had a job to do and she was comfortable he'd do it to the best of his ability. That's all she should care about.

Besides, if she were very lucky she'd be leaving his ranch within the next twenty-four hours at the most. She'd be back enjoying her own life and far away from this man and this godforsaken countryside.

At last, that's what she wanted to believe, but she knew in her heart nothing would be the same in Niflheim. What was happening there? She regretted not being better informed about the political unrest that had exploded.

What about her friends and the palace staff? Were they safe? She had to believe they were, otherwise grief would consume her.

Her irritation with Tanner and the thought of home did nothing to staunch her appetite, and despite the tension-filled silence between them, she enjoyed the cheeseburger and fries and chocolate shake she'd ordered.

Tanner ate more quickly, finishing his meal before she was even half finished. He tapped his fingers on the tabletop, unconsciously signaling impatience, which only made her eat at a more leisurely pace.

"Ever hear of stopping to smell the roses?" she asked.

"I thought you weren't speaking to me," he replied as his fingers stopped their rapid tattoo.

"I wasn't. Now I am." She stabbed a French fry into a pool of ketchup, popped it into her mouth and chewed thoughtfully.

"Can I ask you something?"

"Sure." She ate another fry.

"This morning you said something about I'd better not throw you over my shoulder." A wrinkle furrowed his brow. "What was that all about?"

"I assumed it was a cowboy thing. I watched a Western one time and the cowboy got irritated with the woman and threw her over his shoulder. I just wanted to let you know I won't tolerate such behavior."

One of his dark brows rose. "You don't have to worry. In the movies the cowboy throws the woman he loves over his shoulder."

She paused with a French fry in midair. "I always wondered what happened after that," she mused. "I mean, where does he carry her off to and what do they do?"

He tapped his fingers once again on the tabletop. "It's the movies, who knows?"

She stabbed another fry into the ketchup, ignoring the edge of irritation in his voice. "Who's minding the office today while you're minding me?"

"I have a very efficient receptionist/secretary. Ida Marie will handle things at the office and call me if anything comes up. She's a good woman."

She eyed him curiously. "What makes her a good woman?"

He sat back in the booth. "What do you mean?"

"I mean, what qualities do you think make a woman a good woman?"

"This is a ridiculous conversation," he scoffed.

"It's called small talk. People often do it when they're sharing a meal. Come on, Tanner, pretend for a moment you're a civilized man."

She was aware of the fact that she baiting him and she wasn't sure why. Maybe because of his crack earlier about all play and no work. And maybe because she really wondered what kind of a woman a man like Tanner would respect.

"Ida Marie raised two children as a single parent," he said, apparently deciding to play along. "Before I hired her to work for me she'd done all kinds of jobs— waitressing, housecleaning—whatever it took to keep a roof over her kids' head and put food on their table."

"Is that all that you worship?" she asked. "Work?"

He eyed her with a deceptive laziness. "What do you worship, Anna?"

Before she could reply, the door to the café opened

and a tall, older man in a khaki uniform walked in. Instantly she saw Tanner's tension increase. The muscle in his jaw ticked and his body stiffened a bit.

"Afternoon, Tanner," the man said as he approached their table.

"Afternoon, Sheriff," he replied.

The sheriff swept his hat off his head to reveal a thick head of salt-and-pepper hair. He nodded to Anna. "Ma'am," he said, then looked at Tanner expectantly.

"Anne, this is Sheriff Jim Ramsey. Jim, this is Anne Jones, a friend of mine from New York City," Tanner said.

"New York. You're a long way from home, little lady." He looped his thumbs into his thick black belt and rested his arms on his protruding stomach as he eyed her with brown eyes filled with open curiosity.

"She's just visiting the family for several days," Tanner replied smoothly.

"I see." He looked from Tanner to Anna. "First time here in Cotter Creek?"

"Yes, first time," she replied.

He rocked back on his heels, his gaze returning to Tanner. "Not going to be any trouble, is there?" His gray eyebrows danced upward on his broad forehead.

"Not planning on any," Tanner replied.

"Good. Good. You know I like my town nice and quiet. Nice meeting you, Anne." He nodded to Tanner, then turned and headed toward the counter where he sat on one of the stools, his back to them.

Anna looked at Tanner curiously. There had been a subtle tension between the two men. "You don't like Sheriff Ramsey?" she asked softly.

He hesitated a moment, his eyes darkly shadowed and impossible to read. "He's all right. He and his men have worked with me on occasion. You ready to go?" He pulled his wallet from his pocket and placed several bills on the table.

She nodded and together they got up and left the café. "But, you don't really like him," she said, trying to understand the tension that had existed between the two men.

He frowned. "Sheriff Ramsey was the one who notified us of my mother's death," he said as they walked toward the pickup. "Of course, at that time he wasn't the sheriff, he was just a young deputy. He was the first one on the scene and, unfortunately didn't secure the area and evidence was compromised."

Anna wondered what it would be like to see on a daily basis the bearer of such bad news. "And that's why you don't really like him?"

He sucked in a deep breath and put his hat on his head, effectively shielding his eyes with the shadow of the brim. "It's not that I don't like him. The more successful we've become, the more concerned Jim had become about us bringing problems to Cotter Creek. But he can't really complain, we rarely bring trouble here. In fact, you're the first client we've had in a couple of years that is staying on the ranch."

They got in the truck and headed back to the ranch. Anna had a feeling this would be the last that she saw of the small town. If her father came for her this afternoon, they would leave immediately. If he didn't come for her immediately, she had a feeling Tanner wouldn't be eager to take her back to town no matter what she needed or wanted.

"When we get back to the house you'll need to find something to do while I spend a little time on the Internet," he said. "I want to see if I can find out something about a group called something of the Mist."

"I could help you," she said. The last thing she wanted was to be sent to her room like a recalcitrant child.

"You can help me by leaving me alone for an hour or two."

"And what am I supposed to do in that time?" she asked.

"I don't know...watch television, read a book. If you really get bored you could ask Smokey if there's something you can help him do with dinner preparations."

"It's bad enough I have to put up with your disrespect. I certainly don't intend to put up with that man's disagreeable nature," she exclaimed as she thought of the man who owned the kitchen.

"I need an hour, two at the most. Surely you can entertain yourself for that length of time."

"All right." She sighed. "I'll be a good girl and entertain myself while you work. But when you're finished, then you have to do something for me."

He released a sigh twice as long as hers. "What?"

She snapped a finger against the brim of her hat. "If I'm going to dress the part of a cowgirl, then the least you can do is show me around the ranch."

He raised a dark eyebrow. "You sure you want to do that? You're liable to get your boots dusty."

"I don't mind. I've never been on a ranch before and I'd like to see everything."

He frowned and didn't answer for a long moment. "All right, after I take care of my business, I'll give you a little tour of the place," he agreed.

The rest of the drive was accomplished in a silence that he didn't seem inclined to fill. Once again she found herself sneaking glances in his direction. Today he wore a short-sleeved, light blue shirt, the color transforming his eyes to a blue-green mix.

Anna had dated plenty of men, but none as handsome as Tanner and none who had the power with a mere glance of eyes or a curve of lips to accelerate her heartbeat and make her feel both excited and anxious at the same time.

Earlier, when he'd adjusted her hat, there had been a moment when she'd thought he was going to kiss her, when she'd wanted him to kiss her. But that was crazy. Why would she want a man who managed to make her feel both anxious and slightly inadequate to kiss her?

She didn't even know Tanner. He meant nothing to her, and as soon as her father came for her, he would be nothing more than a memory to store away forever.

They had just entered when Red came out of the study. "Anna, your father is on the phone."

She raced to the study and grabbed up the receiver. "Father!"

"Anna, my dear. I'm so glad you managed to get to safety. I was worried you'd not be able to handle yourself." His familiar voice filled the line and she closed her eyes as a wave of deep relief swept over her.

Even though the news sources had indicated that nobody had been hurt in the shoot-out in L.A., she'd needed to hear her father's voice. She'd needed to know for herself that he was truly all right.

"I'm here… I'm fine," she replied, aware that Tanner had entered the study and was standing just inside the doorway. She gripped the receiver tightly against her ear. "Where are you? What's happening? When are you coming here for me?"

"I need to speak with Tanner West, Anna."

"But Father—"

"Anna, this is important business. Don't you worry yourself. Everything will be just fine, but I need to speak to Mr. West right now." His voice was firm and sharp.

A burning sting of unexpected tears sprang to her eyes as she realized she'd been summarily dismissed. Without another word she handed the phone to Tanner and hurried from the study.

She went directly to her bedroom, needing a few minutes alone. Standing at the window, she stared outside where thick, heavy, dark gray clouds were gathering in the distance. It felt as if they were a reflection of the heavy grayness of her heart.

She adored her father and knew that he loved her, too, but this wasn't the first time he'd hurt her feelings. He rarely had time for her, but she'd always understood that he was an important man.

Still for most of her life he had dismissed her as a pretty, empty-headed bauble. The telephone conversation she'd just had with him had merely served to emphasize their relationship.

She'd been sheltered from the dark side of power, but she'd allowed it, and she had to take a certain amount of responsibility for not knowing what had been happening in Niflheim before the coup. She recognized now that knowledge was a good thing and if she'd really been a good princess she would have educated herself despite her father's sheltering ways.

Her father was a good man, but she had a feeling he'd been a king out of touch with what his people wanted, what they needed. She hoped he was doing some serious soul-searching that would result in making him a better king…if he got the opportunity to return to Niflheim.

The future loomed before her, dark and uncertain. What would become of her father if he couldn't go back to his country? Would he abdicate his throne and live the remainder of his life in hiding? What was her future? Would peace be returned to Niflheim? So many questions and so few answers.

A knock fell on her door. Quickly she wiped the tears that had gathered at her eyes and opened the door. Tanner eyed her closely. "Are you all right?" He shoved his hands into his pockets and looked ill at ease.

"Of course I'm all right," she said too quickly.

"Well, I have good news and bad news," he said. "The good news is your father is fine. The bad news is he wants you to remain here and it will be a week, possibly two, before he can come here to get you."

"A week or two?" She sank onto the edge of her bed.

"It looks like we're stuck here and we'll just have to make the best of the situation. I'm going to check out what I can find about those rebels. When I'm finished, I'll give you that tour we talked about."

"No, that's all right. I've changed my mind," she said. "I'd rather not get all dirty and icky." She thought she saw a shadow of disappointment in his eyes. She didn't care. She was everything he thought she was…a spoiled, lazy, overindulged young woman. "I'll just hang out here and do my nails or something until dinnertime."

"Fine. I'll see you at dinner." He closed the door, but not before she saw the disgust in his eyes.

# Chapter 5

The thunder awakened him, but it was the scream that followed that shot him out of bed. He grabbed his gun from the nightstand and bolted toward the bedroom door.

It had been Anna's scream. And the fear that ripped through his veins was as electric as the lightning that flashed, illuminating the night sky.

As he left his room a hundred questions ran through his mind. Had he underestimated the enemy? Not taken the necessary security measures? The nightlight burning in the hallway led him to her room.

He didn't bother to knock on her door, but rather threw it open and stepped inside with the gun in his hands and ready for business.

Lightning once again seared through the sky, its brilliance filling every corner of her room. In that flash of light he saw her. It was just a flicker of sight, but it was enough to freeze him in place as thunder boomed overhead.

She sat up in the bed and the sheet was at her waist, leaving her naked from that point up.

. "Tanner," she gasped. Lightning flashed once again and this time he saw that she had grabbed the sheet up to her neck, hiding her nakedness from his eyes.

"Are you all right? I heard you scream." His voice sounded thick and strange to his own ears. That vision of her with her hair wild and tangled and her breasts bare was like a snapshot permanently burned into his brain.

"I—I had a nightmare and the thunder frightened me. I'm sorry. I didn't mean to disturb you."

She had no idea just how much she'd disturbed him. Thunder boomed again and a small cry escaped her. This time when lightning filled the room he saw her eyes, big and round and filled with fear.

"Get dressed and we'll get something to drink and wait for the storm to pass." He turned and headed for his own room, where he put his gun away and pulled on a pair of jeans over his boxers.

And tried to forget the picture of her naked in bed.

He was surprised that the scream hadn't awakened his father or Smokey, but as he walked through the great room toward the kitchen, nobody else stirred in the house.

What he needed was a shot of whiskey or something that would put a fire in his gut that had nothing to do with the one Princess Anna Johansson had lit inside him.

He poured a single glass of milk and set it at the table, then reached into the cabinet where he knew Smokey kept a bottle of whiskey hidden. He poured himself two fingers, then sat at the table to wait for her.

He'd seen little of her that evening. She'd come to the table for dinner and had been unusually quiet. Afterward she had immediately returned to her room.

He had the feeling that something about the phone call from her father had upset her, but the conversation had been so brief he couldn't imagine what had been said to upset her in such a short amount of time.

She was probably devastated to realize she was stuck here for a week or two and had spent that time in her room pouting like a child who hadn't gotten her way. She'd certainly made it clear that she didn't want to be here a moment longer than necessary.

He'd thought she was somehow needling him when she'd told him she slept in the nude, but he knew now she'd been telling him the truth. He turned the glass of whiskey in his hand, wondering how many of them he'd have to drink before that vision of her would blur in his head.

Unfortunately he couldn't afford to have as many as it would take to fuzz his thoughts. It never left his mind that he was on duty twenty-four hours a day.

"I'd rather have one of those than a glass of milk," she said as she entered the room. She gestured to the whiskey he held, then winced as another clap of thunder boomed overhead. She slid into a chair at the table and wrapped her arms around herself.

He nodded and got up to get her a glass. When he returned to the table he poured her a small amount of the amber liquid, then watched as she took a sip.

She was dressed in the same T-shirt and jeans she'd had on earlier in the day and he tried desperately to keep his gaze off her breasts, tried to forget their naked fullness with their dark pink centers.

"I'm sorry I screamed and woke you. It's not just the storm," she said, wrapping her slender fingers around the small glass in front of her. "It's the combination of the storm and the nightmare I was having about that day at the airport and the thunder boomed and in my dream it was a gun shooting and my father was shot and there was blood…." Her voice trailed off and she closed her eyes, as if to steady herself.

For the first time Tanner realized the trauma that she'd suffered in the days before she'd appeared on his doorstep.

She hadn't really talked about the terror of being roused out of sleep and taken away from home.

She hadn't really told him all about that moment in the airport when guns had blazed and bullets had flown. Whatever terror she'd felt had been hidden beneath a layer of attitude.

"It was just a dream," he said, recognizing that his words could do little to help with whatever was going on in her head.

"I know." She opened her eyes and he saw the glimmer of tears. "It was just so awful." She jumped as thunder once again boomed so loud that the windows rattled in their frames. "The thunder sounds like the guns that day at the airport."

She downed the liquor in one swallow and he followed her lead, downing his own as quickly. "You want to talk about it?" he asked, and poured them each another small shot.

She stared down into the glass and turned it slowly in her hands. "It had been such a long flight and my father and I were both exhausted." Her voice was soft and low. "We got off the plane and went to the baggage claim to get our bags."

She paused a moment and twirled her glass between her fingers, then continued. "We got our luggage and followed the signs for ground transportation and had just stepped outside of the airport when the gunmen began shooting."

Her eyes were haunted and she reached a trembling hand across the table toward him. He hesitated only a second, then grabbed her hand in his. So small, he thought. Her hand was so small and soft and trembling, and a fierce, unexpected protectiveness swelled up in his chest.

"Bullets seemed to come from every direction. I

don't know how they managed to miss me, miss my father. I don't know how the rebels didn't kill innocent people with their attack."

"Thank God they didn't."

She squeezed his hand and gave him a forced smile. "Yes, thank God for that. Have you ever been shot at?"

The question let him know she wanted a change of subject. "Once. A couple years ago."

"What happened?" She held his hand tight as if he were her lifeline through the storm and through the darkness of her memory.

"I was acting as a bodyguard for a businessman who had ticked off a nasty ex-con. We were getting into the car one morning and somebody took a shot. It shattered the windshield on the car, but missed us."

"Were you scared?" she asked.

"I'm not the kind of man who scares easily."

"So what happened?" she asked.

"The ex-con wasn't especially bright. Two witnesses saw him take the shot at us. He was arrested, and as far as I know is still in prison for attempted murder."

"You're very brave."

"No more than anyone else," he countered. He was feeling uncomfortable, aware that he was seeing a side to her that he hadn't seen before. It was a softer, more vulnerable side and it was far too appealing for his comfort.

"I was just doing what had to be done," he said gruffly, then pulled his hand from hers and drank the last of the whiskey in his glass.

"What did my father have to say to you?" she asked.

He leaned back in his chair and frowned thoughtfully. "Not a lot. We only spoke for a moment. But he did give me the name of the fanatical rebels...the Brotherhood of the Mist. I spent most of the evening on the Internet trying to find out something about them, but had no luck."

"At least you got that much. It's certainly more than he said to me." She looked down for a long moment, and when she looked back at him her eyes were filled with a soft vulnerability, a deep longing for something. It shook him.

"Your father...is he a good king?"

A tiny frown appeared between her eyebrows. "He's a good man and he wants what's best for the country, but I don't think he's been a man in touch with the people. I think he's ignored the fact that it's time for changes in Niflheim."

"Sounds to me like he can't ignore it any longer," he observed. "What do you want for your country?"

"Me?" She looked surprised, as if nobody had ever asked her opinion before. The frown deepened slightly. "I'm just hoping some sort of compromise can be reached that would allow my father a place and give the people what they want." She shrugged. "Where did you meet my father?"

"A couple of months ago we were both at a fund-raiser in Washington. We found ourselves standing next to each other while we waited to be seated for dinner. I told him about my business and he told me about his connection to my father. He also mentioned his daughter."

"That's surprising," she murmured so softly he wasn't sure he'd heard her correctly.

Again he was struck by how fragile she looked, how lost. "The storm has pretty well passed. You shouldn't have any problems sleeping for the rest of the night." He stood, feeling the need to escape her.

Anna with her pretty blue eyes and winsome smile. Anna with her soft skin and provocative scent. Anna with her full breasts and her bare flesh shining in that flash of lightning. She suddenly scared him more than any bullet he might have to dodge.

She downed her drink without blinking, then stood and carried her glass to the sink. When she turned to face him her eyelids were heavy and, with her tousled hair, she looked sexy as hell.

"Come on, it's late and going without sleep makes me cranky," he said.

"Everything makes you cranky," she replied.

He merely grunted, his blood pressure feeling dangerously high as he followed behind her to the bedrooms. She had a sexy sway to her hips that could torment a man to distraction.

She stopped at her bedroom door and turned to face him, her features illuminated by the night-light that burned in the hallway. "Thank you, Tanner. Thank you for distracting me through the storm."

"It's all part of the job," he said, trying desperately to keep everything on a professional basis. He started to walk away, but stopped as she called his name once again.

"The offer of the tour of the ranch, does it still stand?"

"Sure. We could do it tomorrow."

"I'd like that," she replied, then disappeared into the room and closed her door.

Tanner went to his bedroom, knowing that sleep would be a long time coming. He shucked off his jeans and got back into bed, adrenaline making relaxation impossible.

Thoughts of Anna filled his head, visions of her danced in front of his eyes. He had to remember that bad dreams and a thunderstorm had prompted the softness, the vulnerability, he'd seen moments before.

He had no doubt in his mind that when the sun was shining once again in the morning she'd return to being irritating, outspoken and demanding.

Now if he could just forget how she'd looked in bed.

The alarm clock went off and Anna groaned and threw a hand out to slap at the offending instrument.

She rolled over and sat up, eyeing the clock with malicious intent.

Five-thirty. In her real life she rarely got up before noon.

If she'd been home she would have awakened when she'd felt like it and rung for her personal maid and assistant. Astrid would have come into her bedroom carrying her breakfast on a tray and while Anna ate they would have talked about the plans for the day.

Her automatic response now was to fall back down and go back to sleep, but instead she got out of bed and headed for the shower, determined that she'd be at the table when breakfast was served.

As she stood beneath the spray of hot water, she thought of those moments she'd spent in the kitchen with Tanner the night before.

The storm had terrified her, but she'd been comforted by his calm, steady presence. She tried to forget the vision she'd had of him in that brief flash of lightning when he'd first entered her bedroom.

He'd been wearing only a pair of boxers and he'd stolen her breath away with his half-naked masculinity. She'd wanted to leap out of bed and into his arms. She'd wanted to feel his broad, muscled chest against her bare breasts. She'd wanted to stand up and pull him down on the bed with her.

It must have been the storm and her fear that had created such crazy feelings. She didn't need a man like Tanner in her life, at least not after the potential for danger had passed. She definitely didn't need too many mornings beginning before the crack of dawn.

She dressed and pulled her still damp hair together with a ribbon at the nape of her neck, then left her bedroom and headed for the dining room.

She was surprised to discover herself the first one there. As she stood hesitantly in the doorway, Smokey came in through the kitchen carrying a large platter of bacon and sausage.

"Well, well. Will wonders never cease?" he said as he set the platter on the table. "She's actually going to make a meal on time."

"Oh, stuff it in your ear, Smokey," she muttered, refusing to be intimidated by him.

One of his grizzled gray eyebrows shot up in surprise then a small smile curled one corner of his mouth. "Coffee's coming," he said, then returned to the kitchen.

Before Smokey returned with the coffee, Tanner entered the dining room, looking as crabby as a grizzly bear awakened from his winter's nap.

"Good morning," she said as she sat at her place at the table. "You look like you crawled out on the wrong side of the bed." She smiled at Red, who followed on his son's heels.

Tanner's scowl deepened and before he could say anything Smokey reentered with a pot of steaming coffee. He served Anna first, then Tanner, who threw himself into his chair at the table as if the entire world was an affront to him.

His foul mood didn't seem to ease with the meal. As Anna listened to Red tell her stories about past spring storms, Tanner nursed a cup of coffee, his eyes dark and fathomless.

"So, are we on for the tour of the ranch?" she asked, rising when breakfast was finished.

"I've got some work to catch up on this morning in the study. We'll take the tour after lunch." As he stood, it was obvious his tone of voice brooked no room for argument. "In the meantime, you can go back to bed or count your diamonds or do whatever princesses do in the mornings."

She had no idea what had caused his current mood but was aware that he was dismissing her, just like her father did so often. "A wonderful idea," she said airily. "I'll just crawl back into bed and catch up on my beauty sleep or maybe do my nails. It's a shame there isn't a spa nearby. I don't believe I've ever gone this long without a facial."

That telltale muscle ticked in his jaw. "Stay in the house, stay out of trouble and I'll see you at lunch," he said, then turned and left the dining room.

"He's got his britches twisted in a knot this morning, doesn't he?" Red said as he sipped his coffee.

Anna couldn't help but smile at Red's words. "I've never heard that particular expression before," she said, and once again sat at the table.

"I'd say in this instance it fits." Red shook his head and took another sip of his coffee.

"If I was to guess, he was born with his britches in a knot," she said.

Red grinned, then shook his head once again. "I keep telling him he needs to take some time off, have a vacation and forget the business for a while, but he doesn't listen to me."

"He strikes me as a man who doesn't listen to any-one," she replied.

"He's a tough one, all right. Always has been, even when he was young. But he's a good man. Wild West Protective Services enjoyed a good reputation and a certain amount of success while the kids were grow-ing up, but it was Tanner who took the business by the horns and grew it into the multimillion dollar indus-try it has become." There was an undeniable ring of love and respect in Red's voice. "He's a successful man, but I think he's a lonely man."

If he's lonely, it's his own fault, Anna thought a few minutes later as she left the dining room. He was judg-mental and overbearing. Was it any wonder he didn't have a woman in his life?

She walked to the window in the great room and peered outside. The sun was just peeking over the ho-rizon, sending splashes of pinks and oranges across the sky. The beauty made her breath catch in her throat.

She opened the front door and stepped out onto the wide, wraparound porch, taking in the sweet-scented morning air as she watched the most beautiful sunrise she'd ever seen in her life. The colors were as bright, as pure, as any gemstone she'd ever seen.

Maybe this was why ranchers got up at such an ungodly hour, to enjoy this spectacle of nature. It was worth every minute of sleep she'd missed.

She saw several men walking in the distance and assumed they were hired help for the ranch. They waved and she waved back. Several horses danced in a fenced area, snorting and feisty as if the crisp morning air suited their fancy.

For the first time since arriving, she felt peace filter through her, a peace she couldn't remember feeling for a very long time.

What would it be like to live like this? To wake up every morning to a splendid sky and smell wind-sweetened air? To travel into town every day or two and eat at the café, know people by face and by name?

There was a silence to this life she'd never known before. Even now a stillness surrounded her. Would the quiet of this place calm her or drive her slowly insane? How did the people who lived here handle the quiet?

What was she thinking? This wasn't her life. This would never be her life. Her life was shopping and dancing and playing hostess for dignitaries visiting her country. She frowned. But at the moment she didn't have a country. Instead she had rebels who wanted her dead.

For the first time since the night she and her father

had been whisked out of the palace reality sank in and she realized she had no clue what the future held for her.

It was possible her father intended to see exactly what happened in the next week or two in Niflheim and would decide to make a stand to get his country back. It was also possible they would never return to Niflheim again.

It made her sad just a little, to realize that the thought of never returning to Niflheim didn't bother her too much. Although it was home, it had never really felt like home to her.

Troubled by the uncertainty of the future and her own thoughts, she turned and went back inside and to her room. She sat on her bed and wondered what the future held for her.

She stood and wandered around the room, wondering what women did to pass the time in a place like this? What was she going to do to pass her time here? Tanner certainly didn't seem inclined to entertain her and she'd rather die from boredom than attempt to make small talk with Smokey.

Red was the only person she might have sought out to pass the time, but he had indicated at breakfast that he was heading out for Oklahoma City to a horse auction and wouldn't be home until later in the evening.

By nine o'clock she was bored out of her head and went down the hallway to the study. She knew with the mood Tanner had been in earlier she was taking her life into her hands by disturbing him, but she wondered if he'd learned anything about the group of rebels who wanted her dead.

He looked up from his computer monitor as she entered the room, a frown creasing his forehead.

"Are you going to growl or bite at me?" she asked as she stood in the doorway.

He leaned back in his chair and raked a hand through his thick dark hair. "Depends. What do you want?"

"I'm not sure," she said, sliding into the chair opposite the desk. "I saw the sunrise earlier. Are they always so pretty here?"

The frown across his forehead disappeared. "If you think the sunrises are pretty you should see the stars at night."

"Maybe you'll show them to me some night?"

"Maybe," he replied, his eyes dark and guarded.

She sighed. "So what are you working on?"

He ran a hand across his lower jaw, the frown once again appearing in his forehead. "I spent most of yesterday evening and this morning trying to find out more information about the Brotherhood of the Mist."

"Have you had any luck?"

"No, but I'll tell you what I have discovered. There are hundreds of wacko subversive groups functioning in the world these days. There are religious, political, ecological groups working both inside and outside the law. What I'm not finding is anything new about the situation in Niflheim." He sighed in frustration.

"Why don't you knock off and take me on the tour

before lunch?" she suggested. "It's a beautiful morning, too pretty to be cooped up in here." He hesitated and she knew an automatic protest was about to make its way to his lips. "Come on, Tanner. All work and no play isn't healthy. Besides, don't you want me to say nice things about you and your business after I'm gone?"

"If you can say anything after you've left here, then I'd say I've done my job well," he countered. To her surprise he pushed away from the desk and stood. "All right. I guess I could use a break."

Minutes later with her new hat on her head, Anna followed Tanner out the front door. "There's no sign of the storm from last night," she said as they walked around the house and to the back.

"It was mostly lightning and thunder but very little rain," he replied, his own hat low on his forehead. She saw him nod to a man who stood on the far side of the porch. "So, what do you want to see?"

"Anything…everything," she replied, glad to be outside instead of cooped up in the house. "Is that man one of your employees?"

"Yeah, and there's another one at the back of the house. We'll have guards on the house as long as you're here."

This sobered her somewhat. She'd felt utterly safe here from the moment she'd arrived, but the knowledge that there were two men on guard duty reminded her that danger could find her.

"We'll start in the stables," he said. "Do you ride?"

"It's been years. My mother loved to ride and when I was little we'd often ride together. After her death my father sold all the horses." She remembered that day, with her heart still grieving for her mother, her beloved pony had been sold and taken away.

"Maybe while you're here we'll get you up on a horse again," he said.

"I'd love that."

They entered the stables and her nose was assailed by the scents of horse and leather and hay. They were greeted by soft whinnies and pawing from the stalls. Anna walked to the first stall and turned to face Tanner. "I'll ride this one," she said, indicating the large brown horse.

"Yeah, you'd last about a minute on his back." He pointed to the next stall. "If you ride, you'll ride Molly."

She stepped in front of the next stall to see a smaller brown horse with a white marking on her forehead. "Molly. Hey, pretty lady," she said, and rubbed her fingers over the horse's forehead. She turned back to Tanner to see him wearing a deep frown. "What's wrong?"

"Her stall. It needs mucking out."

"Mucking out? What does that mean?"

"The old bedding needs to be removed and new bedding put in."

"Then why don't you do it?" she asked.

He tipped his hat back from his forehead. "Why don't you?" he countered. His eyes glittered with challenge.

"You don't think I can?" She looked at the stall floor. It couldn't be that hard to remove the straw that was there and put down some new straw. He thought she couldn't do it. He thought she couldn't do anything.

He walked over to the wall and retrieved a pick and a shovel and returned to where she stood. He held out the tools, an amused grin on his face. "Princess, I don't think you'll last five minutes."

"Start your clock, pardner," she replied, and took the pick and shovel from him.

## Chapter 6

Tanner almost felt guilty as he handed her a pick and a shovel, then moved Molly into an empty stall. Mucking out a stable was one of the nastiest jobs there was and certainly not work befitting a princess.

As he got a wheelbarrow to carry away the old bedding, he recognized that he'd baited her into this particular challenge because he'd been in a foul mood.

His mood had been the result of an endless night of tossing and turning and dreaming about a very naked Anna in his arms.

He'd been angry with her for being tempting and alluring and yet everything he did not want in a woman. This little challenge, which he was certain she would fail, would merely serve to prove to him that she was all wrong for him despite his intense physical desire for her.

He watched her start to work, wielding the pick with her slender arms. Her jeans pulled taut across her bottom as she bent over and he tried not to think about the fantasies he'd entertained the night before.

She flashed a glance at him and gave him a cocky smile. The light blue T-shirt she wore made the blue of her eyes all the more startling.

She could look cocky now, but she'd only been working for three minutes. He fully expected her within the next couple of minutes to stomp her foot and announce that she was finished, that this kind of physical labor was beneath her.

That kind of a reaction would make it easy for him to remember that she was nothing more than a spoiled, pampered princess who wouldn't know the pleasure of a day's work if her life depended on it.

"Had enough?" he asked as she dumped her third shovel full of old bedding into the wheelbarrow.

Her eyes sparked with stubbornness. "It's not finished, so neither am I." She got back to work.

Flies buzzed in the air and the temperature in the stable began to climb. She threw off her hat and he saw that dots of perspiration had appeared on her forehead. She didn't talk, which was a miracle in itself.

In the time they had spent together he'd found her

to be annoyingly chatty. But now it was as if the physical labor took too much out of her for her to work and
carry on a conversation.

His guilt nearly choked him. What did he think he
was doing letting her work like this? What kind of perverse notion had even led to this challenge?

"I could give you a hand," he offered, and reached
for the shovel leaning against the stall.

She whirled around, wielding the pick like a
weapon of mass destruction and glared at him. "Don't
you dare touch that shovel. I don't want your help. I
don't need your help." She set down the pick and
grabbed the shovel and filled it once again.

"You'd love that, wouldn't you," she muttered
under her breath. "You'd love it if I'd grab my crown
and run to my room."

"Anna…"

"Don't 'Anna' me," she exclaimed. "I'm going to
finish this work and in turn you're going take me for
a horseback ride and you're going to sing a cowboy
song and not think about work for at least an hour."

He grinned, amused by her list of demands. "If I
were to sing a cowboy song you really would grab
your crown and run to your room."

She leaned against the shovel, looking as charming
as he'd ever seen her. Several pieces of straw clung to
her hair and a smudge of dirt darkened one cheek.
"That bad, huh?"

"Tone deaf," he replied. "Stone-cold tone deaf.

Anna, you've proved your point, there's no reason for you to finish this."

"I need to do this, Tanner." She frowned thoughtfully. "I'm not sure why, but I need to do it all by myself. But, I'm serious about that horseback ride."

"It's a deal," he agreed. "We'll ride right after lunch."

At heart he liked to think he was a gentleman, and standing around watching a woman work wasn't his idea of fun. He wasn't even sure now why he'd challenged her, what he'd hoped to prove.

She worked until she was half breathless and her arms trembled from over-exertion. Not a word of complaint spilled forth from her and Tanner felt a grudging admiration for her tenacity.

When she had the floor of the stall cleaned, he ignored her protests and helped her put down new bedding. When they were finished she leaned on the handle of the shovel and pushed a strand of her golden hair away from her glistening face.

"I can work," she said. "Nobody's ever expected me to before. Nobody has ever let me before." She leaned the shovel against the wall. "And now, I'm going to take a long hot shower before lunch."

He walked just behind her toward the house, wondering if he hadn't drastically underestimated her character. As she headed down the hallway toward her bedroom, he went into the kitchen where Smokey was busy with lunch preparations.

"You've been scarce this morning," Smokey said.

"I've been teaching Anna how to be a cowgirl."

Smokey snorted. "And next week you can teach me how to be king."

Tanner smiled wryly. "I think I'd have far more luck transforming Anna into a cowgirl than I could have trying to turn you into a king. She spent the morning mucking out a stall."

Smokey raised a grizzled eyebrow. "Maybe there's more fiber to the woman than I first thought. She's a feisty one, that's for sure. Damned if she didn't tell me to stick it in my ear this morning."

"Now that doesn't surprise me," Tanner replied. "She doesn't take any guff from anyone. Don't set the table for me and Anna for lunch," he said as an idea struck him.

"You're not eating?" Smokey asked.

"I promised her we'd take a horseback ride. I think I'll just throw a couple sandwiches in a bag and we'll have a picnic while we're out."

"A picnic?" Smokey looked at him as if he'd just grown a second head.

"Don't look at me as if I've lost my mind," he said irritably. "It's for her, not me. I'm just going along for the ride." Tanner walked over to the refrigerator and pulled it open.

"Go on, get out of here." Smokey flicked a dish-towel at him. "You want a picnic lunch, I'll make you one, but don't go pawing around in my refrigerator. I hate it when people paw around in my refrigerator."

Tanner started to reply but was interrupted as his cell phone rang.

"Tanner," he said into the small phone. It was his brother Zack checking in from his assignment in Oklahoma City.

He'd just finished up with the call when Anna entered the kitchen, bringing with her the clean scent of soap and shampoo and the spicy perfume he couldn't seem to get out of his head.

"You're going on a picnic," Smokey said to her.

She looked at Tanner for confirmation. "Really?" He nodded and delight lit her face. "A ride and a picnic? What a wonderful idea."

"Why don't you two go saddle up and I'll bring your lunch out to you," Smokey suggested, obviously eager to get them both out of his kitchen.

"If I'd known that my mucking out a stall would make you so agreeable I would have done it on the day I first arrived here," she said to Tanner as they headed back outside.

"I'm not a disagreeable man," he replied.

She grinned at him slyly. "No, you're quite agreeable when you get your own way and are in total control of things."

"Speaking of control, there are some things we need to go over before we take this ride."

She rolled her eyes. "Let me guess. Rules. Rules for trips into town, rules for eating lunch, rules for horseback riding. I suppose you even have rules when you make love to a woman."

"Don't be ridiculous," he replied. The woman was impossible. Just when he was feeling inclined to be kind to her, she managed to do or to say something to irritate him. After spending the night fantasizing about making love to her, the last thing he wanted to do was to talk about making love.

"I'll bet I know the rules already. Whatever happens, I do exactly what you tell me to do, exactly when you tell me to."

He nodded. "Hopefully these are rules that will keep you alive, Anna."

By the time he saddled up their two horses, Smokey brought them out their lunch. It took only minutes for Tanner to store the bottled water, fresh fruit and sandwiches in his saddlebag, then he watched as Anna mounted Molly.

She looked right on the back of a horse. However, Tanner had yet to see her in any position where she didn't look right. He frowned and mounted his own horse, a black, high-spirited gelding named Simon.

At least with them each on horseback he couldn't smell the provocative scent of her, couldn't see the silver flecks that made her blue eyes interesting as well as pretty.

"Where are we headed, pardner?" she drawled as if she'd been born and raised in Texas.

He couldn't help the smile that curved his lips. She

was irrepressible. "Just riding. No special destination." However, he didn't intend for them to go too far from the house.

Over the course of the past forty-eight hours he'd begun to think that she really might have lost her pursuers in Los Angeles, that she was safe here and he was baby-sitting more than protecting, waiting for her father to arrive.

Besides, there were plenty of ranch hands on the property and they would recognize any strangers that strayed onto the West land. He decided to keep the guards on the house. A short ride on the property should be fine.

Although Simon would have loved a swift gallop, Tanner kept tight control, forcing the gelding to a sedate walk. He had no idea what kind of riding skills Anna might possess and until he did know intended to take it nice and slow.

"Looks like you're going to meet another member of the West family," he said as they headed toward the pasture.

"Really? Who?"

"Zack. He called earlier to tell me that his client has released him and he's returning in the morning."

"What kind of an assignment was he on?"

"The kind we hate to take. A domestic case."

"Domestic case, what does that mean?"

"A husband and wife. The wife wanted a divorce, the husband didn't. It seems he has a temper. Zack was hired to keep an eye on the wife between the time the divorce papers were served to the husband and the trial date, which was today."

"And so the danger to the client is over?"

"She thinks so. Apparently her ex-husband has left town and so she's confident everything will be fine." What he didn't tell her was that there had been something in Zack's voice that had made him wonder if perhaps his brother had gotten a little too close to his client.

Always a mistake, he reminded himself.

As they headed down the lane she asked about the various outbuildings they passed. He explained what each building was and what it was used for. As they passed the original homestead, he told her that it was where he now lived.

"It's very nice," she said. "In fact, it's quite lovely."

"Thanks. I've put a lot of work into it." A sense of pride filled him as they rode past the attractive ranch house. "I've been updating it for the past couple of years…new wiring and new plumbing."

"How many bedrooms does it have?" she asked.

"Three."

"Big enough for a family. How many children do you want?"

"A boy and a girl would be nice." He tried not to notice how the sun sparkled on the ends of her hair beneath her hat. The golden strands seemed to beckon for his touch. "What about you?" he asked, trying to keep his mind focused on the conversation at hand.

"At least two…a boy and a girl. I wouldn't want to have an only child. It's far too lonely." Her expression darkened and she leaned forward to pat Molly's mane.

"From what I've seen of your life you didn't look too lonely to me. I'm sure you have lots of friends." He thought of the pictures of her surrounded by beautiful, wealthy people such as herself.

"Friends? I don't know if I had any or not. That's the problem with being a princess. When I told a joke, everyone laughed whether it was a good joke or not. When I had an idea, it was the best idea anyone ever had. When I wore a dress, everyone said it was the prettiest one in the room. Now I'm sure at one time or another I told a bad joke, had a bad idea and wore an ugly dress, but nobody would tell me because of my position, because of who I was. Were those people friends?"

It was a rhetorical question and he didn't even try to answer it. What surprised him was the touch of sadness he heard in her voice. "You tell a bad joke, don't expect me to laugh. You have a bad idea, I'll be the first one to tell you. You wear an ugly dress and I'm not taking you out in public."

She flashed him a smile, a beautiful, open smile that set a fire in the pit of his stomach. "Ah, he has a sense of humor after all."

Tanner returned her smile. It felt as if it had been years since he'd really smiled at anyone. Months of stress melted away from him. "Of course I have a sense of humor."

"You should show it more often," she exclaimed.

They rode in silence for a few minutes and Tanner felt himself relaxing with each step of the horse. Maybe he had been working too hard lately, not taking any time at all to just enjoy being alive.

"This was a good idea," he said. "I needed to get out and enjoy a ride."

"Do you ride every day?" she asked.

"I used to, but lately it seems there's too much work at the office to do." He'd noticed that she sat the saddle like a natural, that whatever training she'd had as a young girl was evident in the easy way she controlled Molly. "Feel like a run?" he asked.

She flashed another of her smiles. "Just lead the way, pardner."

With a touch of his heels and a loosening of the reins, Simon took off and Molly followed. As far as Tanner was concerned there was nothing more liberating than a run, with the sun warming his shoulders and the scent of pasture filling his lungs.

He kept the gelding reined in enough that Molly could stay abreast. The mare didn't have the long legs or the strength of his horse.

He tried without success to keep his gaze off Anna. The air had whipped color into her cheeks and the hair beneath her hat was tangled and wind-whipped. Her breasts moved up and down beneath her T-shirt as the horse ran.

The subtle embers of desire that had burned in his

stomach from the moment he'd first seen her burst into flames. If he'd been by himself, he would have urged Simon faster, as if to outrun an emotion he didn't want to feel.

Maybe what he felt in his the pit of his stomach nothing more than his appetite? He hoped whatever Smokey had packed for lunch sated that burning hunger.

The gallop invigorated Anna and reminded her of when she'd been little and she and her mother had ridden on the palace grounds. Her mother had been happiest, it seemed, when she'd been on the back of a horse. She'd given the gift of the love of riding to her daughter. Those childhood days had been the happiest Anna had ever known.

Funny that she'd felt almost happy when she'd been shoveling horse manure earlier. There had been a profound sense of accomplishment inside her when she'd finished the test and the fresh bedding had been put down. Who would have thought it?

She was a little bit disappointed when Tanner slowed once again and the horses fell into an easy side-by-side walk.

"I'd forgotten how much I love riding," she said, and tipped her face up toward the midday sun.

"It's one of the simple pleasures of life."

She turned her head to look at Tanner, wondering if he was digging at her once again. But he wasn't looking at her, rather he seemed to be scanning the area around them.

"Everything all right?" she asked, a touch of worry filtering through her.

His gaze flickered to her and he smiled. "Everything seems to be fine. You ready for lunch?"

Beneath the power of his easy smile her worry found no food to sustain it and disappeared. She shook her head. "Not yet. I'm enjoying the ride too much to stop."

For the next few minutes they rode in silence. It was a pleasant silence and Anna found herself looking at Tanner over and over again.

He fascinated her every bit as much as he irritated her. There was a steadiness about him that was comforting, a sense of purpose and drive that intrigued her. In the brief time she'd been in his care she'd come to trust him implicitly.

He'd surprised her the night before with his gentle understanding of her fear of the storm. She remembered the feel of his hand wrapped around hers. His hand had been warm and comforting as the thunder had roared overhead.

He sat tall in his saddle, like a man confident with who he was and how he was living his life. He seemed to know exactly where he was going in life. Unlike her. She had no idea what she was doing or where she was headed.

"It's so quiet out here," she said, needing, wanting

any kind of conversation to take her out of the doubts and worries her thoughts had produced. "That's one of the things I've noticed in the time I've been here."

"Quiet?" He tilted his head and gazed at her quizzically. His lips turned up at one corner in a half smile. "Maybe it's quiet to a woman who's accustomed to loud music and jet engines and the ring of cash registers, but it's not quiet to me. You just don't know how to listen. Tell me what you hear right now."

It was her turn to tilt her head and listen. Certainly there was no music, no ca-ching of a cash register and no traffic noise. "I hear the sounds of the horses' hooves…a bird singing somewhere nearby. A cow mooing." She was surprised at what she heard now that she was really listening.

"The sounds of nature, that's what you hear out here in God's country. Nothing artificial about it. You can hear nature at work. I don't think it's quiet. I think it sounds like home."

*Sounds like home.* What a nice way to think of it, she thought. When she thought of home no particular sounds came to mind except the silence of loneliness.

"You think your father will fight to get his country back?"

"I can only venture a guess," she said thoughtfully. "Even though the rebels appear to be in power at the moment, I'm not sure how long that power will last. My father was not a king without influence, without supporters."

"So tell me, how does a princess spend her days?" he asked as the horses continued to walk side by side.

She frowned thoughtfully before replying. "I know what you think…that I probably slept late, got breakfast in bed, spent the afternoon in a spa or shopping, then partied all night."

"So, tell me differently," he replied.

She straightened in the saddle and thrust her shoulders back, eyeing him from beneath the brim of her hat. "I can't. That's exactly the way I spent many of my days as a princess." She thought she saw a tinge of disappointment in his eyes. "I won't apologize for living out what was expected of me," she continued defensively. "There's no way you could understand my life."

"Why? Because I'm just a dumb cowboy?" There was an edge of defensiveness to his voice.

"I didn't say that."

"But secretly you think that," he said.

"Maybe I did the first time I saw you, but I know differently now. And why are you trying to pick a fight with me?" she asked with a flash of impatience. "You do one thing nice for me, arranging a ride and a picnic, and now you seem determined to ruin it by provoking me into an argument."

"I'm not—"

Whatever he had been about to say was lost beneath the sound of a loud crack.

Molly reared up on her hind legs with a frantic

whinny. Anna tried desperately to hang on as the horse reared again.

"Anna!"

She heard Tanner cry her name as she felt herself falling from the horse. She hit the ground with a painful thud, landing on her backside as the back of her head crashed on the hard earth.

# *Chapter* 7

Tanner flew off Simon as Molly took off in a panicked run. Tanner didn't just crouch next to Anna—he threw his body over hers, his gun drawn and his gaze focused on the trees in the distance.

His heart thundered in his chest as he glanced at Anna, grateful to see her eyes open and looking at him. He'd been afraid she'd been hit when he'd seen her body fall like a rag doll from Molly's back.

"Are you all right?" he whispered. He didn't look down at her again but rather kept his attention riveted to the copse of trees.

"I—I think I'm okay. I hit my head…that's all. What…what happened?"

"Somebody took a shot at us. I think the bullet must have hit Molly."

"Oh, no. We have to find her." She pushed against his chest, but he remained flat against her, his weight making it impossible for her to move.

"We're not going anywhere until I'm certain whoever took that shot isn't waiting to take another one."

"But, Molly…"

"She'll head back to the stable."

Dammit, the trees were just thick enough to provide ample cover for a gunman. Was somebody still there waiting to take another shot at them? At Anna?

"They found me," she whispered, her terror obvious as her fingers clutched at his back.

"We don't know that." He shot a quick look at her. "You hear me? We don't know that for sure. It could have been a hunter." He said it for her benefit, but he knew it wasn't hunting season and nobody in their right mind would be hunting on West property.

"A hunter?" Hope lightened her voice. "What are we going to do?" she asked.

"We're going to wait." He kept his gaze on the trees, cursing himself for not sensing any danger. Even now he saw no hint of anyone hiding in the thick brush. No flash of color from clothing, no glint of a shotgun barrel peeking out. Nothing.

Minutes ticked by and Tanner remained on the ground, his body covering hers. As the initial wave of shock passed, he became acutely aware of every point of contact his body had with hers.

His chest mashed against her breasts, his groin against hers. Despite the reason for their present position, a crazy heat swept over him.

He ignored it and focused on the problem at hand. And the problem was he didn't know what they were up against. He had no idea if the shooter was still in the trees. He had no idea if there was more than one shooter. He just didn't know what in the hell they might be facing.

The fact that no other shots had followed confused him. The fact that they had missed Anna, who had been an upright target in the saddle, also confused him. An assassin rebel with a bad aim?

"Whoever was there, I don't think they're there any longer," he finally said.

"How do you know?" she asked.

"I don't know for sure, but Simon doesn't seem to be sensing anyone in the area."

The big horse stood grazing in the nearby distance. "So, how can we be sure?" Her voice was half breathless.

He looked down at her again. "I'm going to rise. If somebody is hiding in those trees and waiting to take a shot, they'll probably take a shot when I get up."

"Then don't get up," she replied in horror. Her arms tightened around him as if to keep him on top of her.

He offered her a tense smile. "We can't exactly stay here for the rest of our lives."

"I guess this means our picnic is off."

She was impossible. They'd just had a close encounter with a bullet and she was worried about a damned picnic. "I'd say that's the smallest of our problems."

She reached up with one hand and touched his cheek. "Be careful," she said.

In that instant, with her body warm beneath him and her eyes large and luminous, he wanted nothing more than to crash his mouth to hers, to taste those lips that had tormented him to distraction since the moment she'd charged into his office.

But he was her bodyguard, not her lover, and at the moment his job was to keep her protected from harm, harm that had come much too close for his comfort.

In one smooth movement he raised up into a crouch over her. "Stay down," he commanded, grateful that for once she didn't argue or make any movements to protest his command.

Muscles tensed with expectation, he slowly straightened to a standing position. Nothing. No shot, no sound. Nothing happened.

"Simon," he called softly, then whistled. The horse raised its head and whinnied, then ambled over to where he stood. He grabbed the reins and positioned the horse between Anna and the stand of trees.

At that moment the sound of hooves thundered against the earth. Burt Randall, one of the men who'd been on guard duty, came into view, riding fast toward them. He reined in as he reached them, his gaze dark, a line of worry deep across his forehead beneath his worn dark hat.

"You okay?" he asked.

"I think so. How did you know to come find us?" Tanner asked.

"Molly showed up at the stables. I knew the two of you had taken off earlier and something must have happened."

"Somebody took a shot at us," Tanner said. He leaned over and held out his hand to help Anna up careful to keep Simon as a barrier between her and the trees.

Burt touched the butt of the shotgun that lay across his lap. "Where did it come from?"

"Those trees." Tanner pointed.

"I'll go check it out."

Tanner nodded, knowing that the man could take care of himself. "I'm going to get Anna back to the house."

As Burt took off in the direction of the trees Tanner turned to Anna. "It should be safe for you to mount. Whoever was in those trees, if they're still there, they should be running to escape Burt." He motioned her to the horse's back.

She stepped into the stirrup and pulled herself up on Simon's back. Immediately Tanner mounted and, with his arms around her, urged Simon toward home.

She took her hat off and held it in front of her, then

leaned back against him. He wrapped one arm around her and held his gun in the other.

He was relatively certain the danger had passed, knew that Burt had his back. But with each step Simon took toward home, he relived that terrifying moment of watching Molly rear and Anna fall to the ground.

He'd feared she was dead. He'd been terrified that he'd screwed up and Anna had paid for his mistake with her life.

The ride had been foolish. He should have known better than to take her out in the open where she could be a potential target. He'd allowed himself a moment of softness and that moment had almost gotten her killed.

He could smell her hair, the clean scent of sunshine and shampoo. Her body was warm against his and despite all that had happened, she stirred him.

He tightened his arm around her, thinking of how close they had come to catastrophe, how close he had come to losing her. What had he been thinking? How could he have taken such a chance with her, especially not knowing what he was up against?

The stables came into view, but still his nerves felt strung as tight as he'd ever felt them. For now, she was safe, but a deep dread kept at bay any real feelings of relief.

"There won't be any more rides," he said as they dismounted. "In fact, I don't want you outside at all. I don't want you standing on the front porch, in the doorway or peeking out a window."

She eyed him solemnly. "So you don't think it was a hunter after all," she said.

He didn't hold her gaze, but instead led Simon to his stall. "I didn't say that," he replied. He didn't want to worry her, but in his gut he just couldn't believe that the shot was accidental.

"Then why are you saying that I have to stay inside?" She tossed her hat back on the top of her head and peered up at him. "Do you often have problems with hunters?"

"Never," he admitted truthfully as he secured the big gelding in his stall.

"Tanner West, I demand that you tell me what you're thinking," she exclaimed. "I have a right to know what you think."

He whirled around to look at her, his eyes narrowed as the emotions that had roared up inside him at the sight of her falling off the horse spun out of control. "That tone of voice might work on the servants you have back home, but it sure as hell doesn't work on me."

She bit her lip as a wash of pink filled her cheeks. "I'm sorry." She took a deep breath and stepped closer to him, so close he could smell the scent of her, see the silver flecks in her blue eyes. "Tanner, I trust you to tell me what's going on. I need you to be different from everyone else in my life and to tell me what's really going on. I need you to treat me like a competent woman, not like a pampered princess."

"You want me to treat you like a woman?" Somewhere in the back of his mind he knew he was out of control, but at the moment he didn't care.

He grabbed her by her upper arms and pulled her even closer to him. Her soft full lips that had tormented him since the moment he'd met her opened in surprise.

He gave himself no time to think, no time to question his own judgment. Instead, driven by a need more powerful than he'd ever known, he crashed his mouth to hers.

He'd known her lips would be soft. He hadn't expected the heat they contained, a heat that sucked him in, spinning his senses and threatening to buckle his knees.

She didn't fight him, but rather wound her arms around his neck and leaned into him, molding her body to his as she returned his kiss with fervor.

Her hat fell to the ground behind her as he tangled his hands in her hair and reveled in the feel of the soft, silky strands.

He wanted to pull her into a straw-filled stall and make love to her. He wanted to lose himself in the blue depths of her eyes, in the sweet fragrance of her, in the lush curves that confirmed she was, indeed, a woman.

But she was more than a woman. She was a princess. His client. His responsibility. He tore his mouth from hers and stepped back from her, unsure if he was angry at himself for crossing a line or at her for shoving him over that line.

"Get in the house," he ordered, trying not to notice that her lips were red from the kiss they'd shared.

She crossed her arms over her chest and eyed him with a touch of defiance. "I will not. Not until I make sure Molly is all right."

It surprised him, the fact that she'd even thought about the horse. But he needed to get her somewhere safe now. "I'll have somebody check her later. Right now we need to get you into the house immediately."

He took her by the upper arm and led her to the stable door. He paused there, not releasing her. The distance between the house and the stable appeared daunting. A lot of open ground to cover without any protection.

"Tanner, you're hurting me," she murmured. He realized in his urgency he'd been squeezing her arm.

He released her. "Stay here. I need to get Sam's attention." He stepped out of the stable and waved to the man standing on the end of the front porch. Sam Wilson, another valued ranch hand who was as good with his gun as he was with the cattle, caught his gesture and headed toward Tanner.

As Tanner waited his mind whirled. He needed to get Anna inside, into an interior room in the house. He had no idea who might be out there, waiting to take another shot, readying for some sort of attack.

"Are you all right, boss?" Sam asked as he reached Tanner.

"Somebody took a shot at us while we were riding.

Burt is out seeing what he can find, but we need to get Anna into the house. I need you to go back to the porch and cover us."

Sam nodded and turned on his heels. As he hurried back to the porch, Tanner could see him turning his head from side to side, assessing the area for an imminent threat.

When he reached the porch he raised his rifle to his shoulder and waited. Tanner turned back to Anna. Her eyes were huge, as if she just now fully understood the danger.

"We're going to walk toward the house," he said. "I'll be directly behind you, covering you like a shield. If anything happens, if you hear gunfire or if for some reason something happens to me, you run for Sam. He'll get you safely inside."

"Okay." Her pulse beat rapidly in the hollow of her throat, belying her calm reply.

"Ready?" Once again he took her arm. Together they left the shadows of the stable and walked out into the sunshine. Although there was some comfort in the fact that there would be few places between the house and the stables for anyone to hide, Tanner couldn't discount the use of weaponry that wouldn't need to put the shooter nearby.

Awkwardly he kept himself as close to Anna's back as he could, alternating between looking ahead and looking back. He didn't breathe a sigh of relief until they hit the porch and she disappeared into the house.

"Thanks, Sam," he said tersely.

Sam didn't lower his rifle. "Nobody is getting through me," he said with determination, displaying one of the reasons he was a trusted employee.

Tanner went inside, to see Anna standing just inside the living room. "Go to the study," he said. The study had no windows, and was an interior room that would be easier to defend if an attack should occur.

"What happens now?" she asked.

"I'm going to call Jim Ramsey and tell him what happened."

"You'll tell him who I am?" she asked as she sank onto the chair in front of the desk.

"No. The fewer people who know who you are, the better. All he needs to know is that somebody took a shot at us." Tanner had learned a long time ago that things went more smoothly if he kept in touch with the local authorities, but as far as he was concerned it was on a need to know basis. "I'll also double the guards around the house."

"What can I do?"

"Stay in here and out of the way," he said curtly. "I'll let you know when the sheriff arrives."

He met Smokey in the hallway and quickly filled the old man in on what had occurred. "I'll get my gun," Smokey said.

Tanner nodded. "Until we know what's going on it would be a good idea if everyone in the house is armed."

It took Tanner only a few minutes to rally more guards and get them stationed around the house. By the time he'd done that, Burt had arrived back at the house.

"I found a couple of cigarette butts just on the other side of the trees," Burt said.

Tanner frowned. "That implies somebody lying in wait. But there's no way anyone could have known I'd taken Anna out for a ride today. I didn't know myself until ten minutes before we went out." He leaned against one of the porch railings, staring out in the distance. "And something else that doesn't make sense is why there was only one shot. If it was some kind of rebel warrior, why not ten shots? Why not a hundred to see that the job got done?"

As he waited for the sheriff to arrive, his mind worked overtime. If the security of this location had been breached, then he needed to move Anna.

Dust in the distance drew his attention and tension ripped through him as he held his gun ready. He relaxed when the car came into view and he recognized it as his father returning from his trip to Oklahoma City.

By the time he'd filled his father in on what was going on, Sheriff Ramsey had arrived. He went back to the study to get Anna and found her sound asleep in the chair.

Oddly enough, he wasn't irritated. Rather he was surprised that she obviously trusted her safety to him enough that she could fall into a deep, easy sleep.

* * *

Anna awoke to a dark room. She sat up and gasped as muscles in her arms, her back and even her neck screamed in protest of any movement.

For a moment she was disoriented, then remembered. The gunshot. The danger. She was in the study and must have fallen asleep while waiting for the sheriff to arrive.

She stood and stretched, then checked the clock on the desk. Just after ten. She'd been asleep for several hours. Wondering what had happened while she'd slept, hunger pangs making her aware she'd missed dinner, she opened the door to the study. She nearly screamed in surprise as she saw Tanner seated in the hallway across from the room.

"You scared me to death," she exclaimed.

He rose to his full height, clad only in a pair of jeans. "Sorry. I was sitting here trying to decide if I should wake you up or just let you continue to sleep."

"I think if I wasn't hungry, I would have slept the night away in that chair."

"Come on, let's get you something to eat and I'll fill you in on what's happened while you slept."

She followed him through the darkened living room to the kitchen, aware that the tension that had emanated from him before seemed to be gone. "Did the sheriff come?" she asked as he gestured her into a chair at the table.

"Yeah, and he gave us some good news." He

opened the refrigerator door and she tried not to notice that he looked as if he'd recently stepped out of a shower. His hair was tousled and slightly damp, and it made her remember the kiss they had shared in the stable.

"What kind of good news?" She couldn't think about the kiss. What she needed to think about was the fact that she'd almost been killed this afternoon.

"The mystery of the gunshot has been solved."

She looked at him in surprise. "What do you mean?"

He didn't answer immediately, but took a moment to slap together a ham sandwich and place it on a paper plate. He set it down in front of her, then slid into the seat next to her.

"Jeffrey Canfield owns the ranch next to ours. Seems his grandson and a friend were out visiting him today. They snuck away from the house and onto our property and spent the afternoon smoking cigarettes and shooting at old tin cans. One of those shots found us."

"So, it wasn't any rebels." A rush of relief swept through her. She picked up the sandwich and took a bite.

"Jeffrey called and apologized, said he intended to tan the hides off the two boys, but I'm just glad to find out it was all an accident." His eyes were the dark green of forest moss, and his expression was serious. "But the same rules apply. I don't want you outside again. We took a chance today and it was foolish, damned foolish."

For some reason she got the impression he wasn't just talking about the horseback ride, but might just be talking about the kiss they had shared, as well.

She took another bite of her sandwich and chewed thoughtfully. It had been a little bit of madness, that kiss. She certainly had no desire to develop any real relationship with Tanner West. Her destiny was not on a ranch with a cowboy, although at the moment she didn't know what her destiny was.

Still, even knowing the kiss had been madness, she wanted a repeat of the insanity. For just that moment when he'd held her so close, when his lips had burned into hers, she'd felt alive for the first time in her life.

As she ate her sandwich he leaned back in his chair and gazed at her with eyes darkly shuttered. She wished she knew him well enough to guess at his thoughts. He looked half angry with her, but that wasn't unusual. Half the time she was around him he looked as if he were angry with her.

A wave of homesickness struck her and she pushed her half-eaten sandwich away, no longer hungry.

"What's wrong? You don't like the sandwich?"

"No, it's fine. I'm just not as hungry as I thought I was. Actually I was just struck by a wave of homesickness."

"Homesick for Niflheim or your lifestyle or what?"

She frowned thoughtfully. "I think I'm mostly homesick for Astrid."

One of his dark eyebrows shot up. "Astrid?"

"She was my personal assistant and maid and as close to a real friend as I had in my life. She'd bring me breakfast in the mornings and we'd talk about anything and everything. Have you learned anything about what happened to the palace staff since the coup?"

"No. I'm sorry."

"What about you, Tanner? Do you have friends?"

"Of course I have friends," he replied quickly, too quickly.

"Really? What are their names?"

He leaned forward, raking a hand through his dark hair. "This is a silly conversation. I have friends. I just don't have a lot of time to spend with them. None of them bring me breakfast in bed and chat about the party I attended the night before."

"Why do you have to do that? Why, when I ask you questions about yourself, do you always have to somehow turn them into an attack on me?"

He sat back once again and averted his gaze. "I wasn't aware that I do that."

"You do, and I'm growing weary of it."

His gaze shot back to her and she saw the narrowing of his eyes. She steeled herself for a retort. Instead he stood and grabbed her plate from the table. "It's late."

She got up from the table and winced as she felt a kink in her shoulder.

"What's wrong?"

"Nothing…I'm just a little sore, that's all." She reached up and touched her shoulder. "I'm not sure whether it's from all the shoveling I did this morning or from my contact with the ground when I fell off Molly."

He frowned, placed her plate in the sink, then walked over to her. "Stand still," he said as he moved behind her. He placed his hands on top of her shoulders and began to knead the muscles.

"Oh-h-h." A soft moan escaped her as his fingers worked the sore muscles, creating a combination of pleasure and exquisite pain. She dropped her chin to her chest to allow him better access.

He had big hands, and by touching her he sent the crazy heat cascading through her again. She knew it was strictly physical. She didn't know him well enough for it to be anything else, but whatever it was, it was wonderful.

"Hmm." Another moan escaped her, and what she wanted to do more than anything was turn around and place her hands on his broad, naked chest. She wanted to touch that wide expanse of tanned skin and muscle, feel the warmth of his skin beneath her fingertips. She wanted him to kiss her again, kiss her long and hard so she could forget everything, especially the danger she'd been reminded today that she was still in.

His ministrations had begun strong and sure, but

had softened, so that it almost felt as if he were caressing her shoulders rather than working out the kinks.

She moaned again and his hands suddenly fell away. She turned, and the look on his face made her breath catch in her chest. Shining from his eyes was a look of hunger. It was there only a moment, then gone.

He stepped back from her and shoved his hands into his pockets. "You might want to take a hot bath to get the rest of the kinks out." His voice was deeper, huskier than usual.

"I'll do that," she said, aware that her voice was more breathless than normal.

"And you'd better get back to bed. Breakfast comes early in the morning." There was a definite edge to his voice.

She stepped closer, reached out and placed a hand on his thick biceps. Just as she'd suspected, his skin was warm and smooth. "Thank you for the sandwich."

She knew she should drop her hand from his arm, but was reluctant to break the physical contact.

"No big deal. But if you don't stop touching me you might get more than you bargained for."

Her heart thrummed in excitement. So, he felt it, too, the crazy pull, the sizzling heat. "And that would be so bad?"

He plucked her hand from his arm. "Lady, that could be downright deadly for both of us." He inhaled a deep, audible breath. "Go to bed, Anna. Your father will be here in the next couple of days and then you can go back to living the lifestyle you had before coming to Cotter Creek."

Moments later, when she was back in her own bed, for the first time since arriving in Cotter Creek the thought of returning to her previous lifestyle didn't excite her but rather filled her with the familiar loneliness and a strange sense of dread.

# Chapter 8

"Is Smokey in charge of changing the sheets on the beds?"

Tanner looked up from the computer to see Anna standing in the doorway of the study. It was after ten. She'd missed breakfast that morning and this was the first time he'd seen her since the night before.

He'd almost been glad he hadn't had to face her first thing this morning. Their middle-of-the-night conversation had disturbed him almost as much as the feel of her slender shoulders beneath his fingertips, almost as much as the silky softness of the ends of her hair against the backs of his hands, the scent of her that had whirled in his head.

"Yeah, Smokey is in charge of clean sheets," he replied, and got up from the desk.

"Don't bother yourself. I'll speak to Smokey about it." Whatever fire he'd seen in her eyes last night was gone, doused beneath a frostiness that was comforting to him.

He had no idea what had caused the distance in her eyes, the coolness in her voice, but he liked it far better than the fire of desire that had lit her eyes the night before.

"I need to take a break anyway," he replied. Besides, he wouldn't miss for the world the princess asking Smokey to change her sheets.

He followed her down the hallway toward the kitchen, trying not to look at the sway of her hips in the jeans that fit her as if she'd been born into them. But, she hadn't been born in denim. She'd been born with a crown on her head, he reminded himself.

Smokey was in the kitchen, cutting up vegetables for lunch. He looked up as they entered, a frown cutting into his forehead. "What is this? A convention of some kind in my kitchen? What do you want?"

"I was wondering when you'd be changing the sheets on my bed?" Anna asked. "It's been several days now. I'm accustomed to them being changed every other day."

Tanner held his breath as Smokey set down his paring knife and wiped his hands on a dish towel. The old man's eyes glittered with a light that Tanner remembered well from his youth, a light that had always made Tanner and the rest of his siblings make themselves scarce.

"You want to know when I'll be changing the sheets on your bed?" he asked.

Anna nodded slowly as if she was aware that she'd made a faux pas but didn't quite know what to do about it.

Smokey disappeared into the laundry room and returned a moment later with a set of clean sheets in his hands. He thrust them toward Anna. "This ain't no full-service hotel and I ain't your personal maid service. You want the sheets changed on your bed, you do it yourself."

Anna glared at Tanner, then at Smokey. "You cranky old toad. You don't have to be so hateful. All you had to do was explain it to me." She turned on her heels and, with all the dignity of a queen, exited the kitchen.

"She's a pain," Tanner said.

"I like her." Smokey looked up to meet Tanner's look of surprise. "Oh, she's spoiled all right, but she's got gumption. She just doesn't know our ways. Can't exactly fault her for being foreign. I 'spect if I went to Paris or some such a place the Frenchies wouldn't quite know what to make of me. I 'spect they wouldn't even know what to make of you."

Tanner grunted, not having a more intelligent reply. As he left the kitchen Smokey's words whirled in his head. Had he been too hard on Anna? Had he not taken into account the fact that she'd been unceremoniously thrust into a foreign lifestyle in a foreign country?

As he walked down the long hallway he heard muttered curses coming from her bedroom. He stepped into the doorway and peered inside to see her wrestling with the bottom fitted sheet. She got one corner beneath the mattress only to have an opposite corner pull free.

"Need some help?" The minute the words left his mouth he regretted them. He wasn't a nursemaid, for crying out loud. He was a bodyguard. Making beds for clients wasn't in his job description.

She looked up at him and blew a strand of her golden blond hair off her forehead. "There's some kind of a mistake. This damned sheet doesn't fit." She glared at him as if he were personally responsible for her being unable to get the sheet on the bed. "Smokey probably did this on purpose, gave me sheets that are too small. He obviously hates me and wants to see me sweat."

"He wouldn't do that. He likes you."

She stared at him with disbelief. "He does not. He's just like you. He thinks I'm stupid and shallow and spoiled." She sank to the edge of the bed. "I can speak five foreign languages, but I can't even get sheets on a bed."

She sounded and looked so miserable, his heart

constricted just a bit. "Why don't I help you with the bed?" he offered.

"If you help me, will you think I'm stupid?"

He smiled at her. "A woman who speaks five foreign languages can't be all that stupid."

She returned his smile and for just a moment there was no tension between them, no underlying friction of any kind. "I would appreciate some help," she finally said grudgingly.

"Come on, it's always easier when there's two people working at it."

It took them only minutes to get the sheets on the bed. As Tanner helped her, he remembered years ago when he'd helped his mother do the same task.

Elizabeth West had been a beautiful woman. Tanner could remember trips into town, where men hurried to nod hello or to open a door for her. Her black hair had been worn long and her eyes had been an emerald-green that had been both beautiful and startling.

"Tanner? Are you all right?"

Anna's voice startled him and he realized he'd been standing still, lost in the memories of boyhood long past. "Yeah, I'm fine. I was just thinking about my mother."

She sat on the edge of the bed once again and this time patted the spot next to her. "What was she like?"

He sank down beside her and for a moment allowed himself to fall back into memories of the woman who had given him birth, the woman who had loved him for the first ten years of his life.

"She was beautiful." Tanner rarely allowed himself the luxury of his memories, but he found himself allowing them now. "She had long dark hair and green eyes and a smile that warmed an entire room. She loved to laugh."

Anna leaned against him, her warmth welcoming. "She sounds like a wonderful person."

"She was. She was strong. Dad was gone a lot and Mom had all of us to contend with, often alone, but I don't ever remember hearing her complain. She loved Dad, loved being our mother, and it showed in everything she did."

"She would have been very proud of the man you've become," Anna said softly. "Your father loved her very much?"

"Very much. I don't think he ever stopped grieving for her." He turned to look at Anna. "I don't think any of us ever really stopped grieving her loss."

He stood abruptly, unwilling to entertain any more painful memories. "Let's get the bedspread on," he said. He walked over and grabbed the bedspread from the floor near the dresser, his gaze falling on a dark blue velvet pouch. "What is this?" he asked.

"My crown. Want to see it?"

He was surprised how much he didn't want to see a reminder of her position, but before he could reply, his cell phone rang.

He held up a finger to indicate she hold on a minute at the same time he answered the call. "Tanner," he said into the receiver.

"She's dead, Tanner. The son-of-a-bitch killed Melissa this morning. He shot her in her driveway then turned the gun on himself." Zack's voice reverberated with all-consuming rage and torment.

Tanner went cold. His breath whooshed out of him as if he'd been punched in the stomach. "Zack…where are you now? Are you still in Oklahoma City?"

"No. I'm an hour out of Cotter Creek." The emotion nearly made his brother's words indecipherable.

"Come straight to the house, Zack. You hear me? Come on in and we'll talk. Dammit," he exclaimed as the line went dead.

"What's wrong?" Anna asked.

"That was Zack. Apparently his client was killed this morning. Her ex-husband killed her, then killed himself."

"That poor woman."

He tugged a hand down his jaw. "Dammit! Zack didn't sound good." His stomach twisted in knots as he thought of his brother. "He got too close to her. I warned him that the first rule in being a good bodyguard was to keep emotional distance between yourself and the client. He didn't listen to me."

"Where's your brother now?"

"He's on his way home, said he was about an hour away. I've got to go speak with my father and Smokey. Will you be all right now?"

"Of course. Go take care of whatever you need to."

He turned and left the room, his thoughts racing. Maybe Zack hadn't been ready for this particular assignment. It had been too long an assignment. Zack had been gone nearly three months.

Zack couldn't blame himself, nor was this a company failure. The client had released Zack. Tanner needed his brother to understand that evil was often more patient than good, that if her ex-husband hadn't killed her today he might have killed her next week or next month or at any time in the future. Zack hadn't failed. He'd kept her from harm until she'd told Zack to go home.

Dammit. He should have sent somebody else, or taken care of it himself. Zack had always been the most emotional of his siblings. Tanner should have known this assignment wouldn't be good for him.

A mistake, and now Zack was hurting as Tanner had never heard him hurt before. Somehow, some way, Tanner had to figure out how to make it all okay.

He found Red weeding in the garden. "Dad, something's happened."

Red stood, the expression on his face letting Tanner know his father's arthritis was bothering him. "What's up?"

"Zack called. All he said was that he's on his way home and his former client was killed sometime this morning. He sounded bad, Dad. I think he got too close."

Red sighed heavily as the two headed back into the house. "We'll get through this, Tanner. We've gotten through worse."

Tanner nodded, wondering what he was going to say to his brother when he had a feeling he was perilously close to making the same mistake with his own client.

Anna sat on the end of the sofa in the great room thumbing through a magazine, aware of Tanner pacing back and forth in front of the windows that looked out to the front of the house.

It had been an hour since Zack had called and Tanner's worry, his tension, seemed big enough to fill the entire house. She wished she knew what to say, what to do to ease his worry, but she didn't have a clue how to help him through this.

Red sat in a nearby chair, staring down at a magazine, but he hadn't turned a page in the past fifteen minutes. Even Smokey occasionally came in from the kitchen to see if Zack had arrived yet.

There wasn't just tension in the room, there was an underlying sense of support, of love, that was almost palpable. It wasn't the first time in the three days that she had been here that she'd noticed the love that was contained within the walls of the house.

At each meal as Tanner and his father talked, Anna had sensed a deep connection between the two men. And whenever Tanner had mentioned one of his brothers or sister, his devotion had been evident in his tone of voice.

What must it be like to be part of such a big support system, to be a part of something so much bigger than one's self? Not as big as a country, which Anna had found impersonal and unfulfilling, but to be a piece of a family who cared about not only your failures, but your triumphs, as well.

She thought it must be an amazing feeling and it was one she hoped one day she would know.

Red stood and Tanner froze as the sound of the crunching of wheels on gravel came through the windows. "He's here," Tanner said softly, his gaze focused out the pane of glass.

Someplace deep inside her Anna knew she should probably retreat to her bedroom and leave this family alone to deal with the situation. She had a feeling there would be pieces to put back together and she really had no place in this family meeting.

But she didn't move from her perch on the sofa as she found herself drawn to the real lives of real people. She realized somehow, some way in the short span of time she'd been in the house, she'd come to care about these people and their lives.

She would have known Zack in a crowd of cowboys. The moment he walked through the front door, she was struck by his close resemblance to his older brother.

He was roughly the same height and body type. Although his hair was longer than Tanner's, it was the same rich dark color and his green eyes stamped him as one of the West children.

Under normal circumstances he was probably quite handsome, but at the moment his features were pulled taut and twisted with raw, naked emotion that was almost painful to see.

"Zackary." Red was the first one to greet him. He wrapped his arms around his son and gave him a bear hug. Zack stood perfectly still in the embrace, neither accepting nor rejecting.

As Red released his son, Tanner stepped toward his brother. "You okay?" he asked.

"Hell, no, I'm not okay." Zack's voice was thick with emotion. "I don't know if I'll ever be okay." He ripped a hand through his hair. "But I'll tell you this. I'm done. I'm finished with all this. I don't want to do this kind of work ever again."

"What do you mean?" Tanner's features pulled into a deep frown.

"What do you think it means? I quit. I don't want to work for you. I don't want to work for the agency anymore."

"That's ridiculous. For God's sake, Zack, give yourself some time." Tanner reached out and placed his hand on Zack's shoulder. "Don't make any decisions while you're upset. You don't want to leave the business. We need you."

Zack jerked away from his brother, his eyes dark

and his mouth a slash of despair. "You know what I need, Tanner? Right now, at this very moment, I need a big brother, not a boss. But I should have known not to expect that from you."

Before anyone could say another word Zack stormed back out the front door and slammed it shut behind him. For just a brief moment Tanner's features reflected a haggard vulnerability, a slicing pain that stole Anna's breath.

It was there only a moment, then gone, replaced by the stoic expression and dark gaze that was so familiar to her. Anna suddenly felt like the intruder she was and she quietly slipped away to her room.

She sat at the foot of her bed and thought about the scene she had just witnessed. What she had just seen was a slice of real life. What she had experienced the whole morning was a vignette of a family.

She'd felt the love and support of Tanner and his father for Zack. She'd felt their worry about him. And she'd seen how people who love one another could hurt and disappoint each other.

Real-life drama, unlike the superficial life she'd led had the capacity to hurt, but it also had the capacity to bring joy and to heal.

There was no way for her to imagine what Zack had been feeling after what he'd been through, but she couldn't forget that moment of stark expression on Tanner's face.

In that unguarded vulnerable moment, she'd seen

that Zack's words had cut him deep and she'd felt Tanner's pain resonating inside of her. It was a strange feeling, that of another's pain. It awed her and made her feel more real than she ever had in her life.

Lunch was difficult. Tension pulsed in the air. Red made small-talk with Anna, but she was acutely aware of Tanner's brooding silence, his dark gaze seemingly focused inward to a place where nobody could follow.

Dinner was a repeat of the uncomfortable lunch. Had Anna not spent the past several days in Tanner's company, she might have thought his dark eyes and tense facial muscles to be solely possessed by anger. But she knew in her heart that it wasn't just anger. It was pain.

That night as she lay in bed sleep remained elusive as she thought of Tanner and his brother. In that moment when Zack had turned angrily on his eldest brother, Tanner had looked as if he'd been slapped.

For the past couple of days Tanner had put his life on hold for her. He'd kept her safe and helped her through the terror of a thunderstorm, had even helped her make the bed where she now attempted to sleep. And now he was all alone in his room and in pain.

Without giving herself a second to think, she slid out of bed, pulled on a T-shirt and pair of jeans and left her room. She padded down the hallway to the room next door, wondering if he was already asleep.

It was possible he wouldn't want to see her, wouldn't want to talk to her. But it was also possible he just might need somebody at this moment. And it surprised her how much she wanted to be the person he needed.

His closed bedroom door should have warned her away, but it didn't. She knocked softly. There was no reply. She knocked again, then took a deep breath, twisted the knob and opened the door.

He stood next to the window, the dim lamp on the nightstand casting him in deep shadows. He wore only a pair of jeans slung low on his hips and his male scent filled the entire room.

He turned to face her. "What do you need, Anna?" His voice was just short of a bark.

For the first time since she'd left her bedroom she realized she had no idea why she was here, why she had felt compelled to come to him. "I'm not sure," she said honestly. "I thought maybe you might need something."

He took a step forward, leaving the shadows of the room behind him. Now she could see the darkness in his eyes, feel the dangerous energy that rolled off him. "You thought I might need something?" He took a step toward her and it wasn't just a feeling of danger that communicated itself to her, but rather a thrum of excitement, as well.

"And just what was it you thought I might need?" he asked as he took another step toward her.

Her mouth dried and her heart began to pound an unnatural rhythm. She was acutely conscious of the bed, mere inches from where she stood, the navy sheets rumpled and the depression of a head still evident on one of the pillows.

She wasn't sure what he needed, but her need for him washed over her. Seeing the way the lamplight played on his bare chest with his scent working its way into her very pores, she felt as if she'd needed him for weeks, months…years.

He dragged a hand through his hair. "Go back to bed, Anna," he said, his voice with a weary rough edge.

She knew she had two choices, to follow his command or to follow her heart. There was really no choice as far as she was concerned.

She took a step toward him. "I don't want to go back to bed. I want to be here with you."

His eyes narrowed and she felt the taut, powerful energy of him sweeping over her. She fought the shiver that tried to crawl up her spine, a shiver of delicious anticipation.

"If you don't leave now, this cowboy won't be responsible for the consequences." There was a distinct warning in his words, but there was also a flame in his eyes that warmed her from head to toe.

"I've never worried much about consequences," she said half breathlessly. "And in this particular case, it's the consequence that I want…that I need."

In three long strides he was in front of her and as he wrapped her in his arms and captured her mouth with his, she knew there was no going back.

## Chapter 9

Tanner knew it was wrong. Someplace in the back of his mind as his arms filled with Anna, as his mouth plundered hers, he knew it was all wrong, but he had no intention of stopping.

The pain of Zack's words retreated as the heat of Anna's mouth suffused him. He knew the pain would return eventually, along with the guilt, but at the moment it was impossible for his mind to entertain anything but the scent and feel of the woman pressed intimately against him.

"Anna," he said as he pulled his mouth from hers. He stared down into her eyes, unsure what he wanted to say. He'd started to warn her that there would be no promises, no future just because of this one night.

But he suddenly recognized he didn't need to tell her that. She was a princess and in all probability the insurgents in her country would be silenced, peace would be restored and she'd return to resume her life. She wasn't about to throw all that away because of one night in bed with a cowboy bodyguard.

She was probably the safest woman he could have a physical relationship with, for she would expect and demand nothing in return.

"Don't talk, Tanner," she replied, her eyes shimmering and luminous. "Don't tell me all the reasons why I shouldn't be in here, why I shouldn't be with you. Just make love to me now."

He certainly hadn't needed any additional encouragement, but her words broke a dam inside him, a dam of want that had been building from the moment she had stormed through his office door.

He crashed his mouth to hers, at the same time his hands moved up beneath her T-shirt to touch the bare flesh of her smooth back. Her skin was like warm satin and electrified his fingertips.

There was nothing soft or hesitant in the way their mouths clung, in the battle of their tongues and the panting breathlessness that seemed to consume them. There was no gentle teasing, no hesitant exploration, only ravenous hunger and clawing need.

There was no bra to encumber him and the thought

of how close he was to feeling those breasts that he'd
seen in the lightning nearly sent him spinning wildly
out of control. He took several deep, steadying breaths
as his hands crept around her and stopped just beneath
the sweet swell of her full breasts. Even though he
hadn't touched her intimately, he could see through her
T-shirt that her nipples were erect as if eagerly anticipating his touch.

He needed to take a moment, wanted to slow down
and to enjoy the journey as much as the final destination. Anna stirred him as he could never remember any
woman doing before her.

Her hands sizzled against the skin on his chest and
as she danced him toward the bed there was nothing
he wanted more than to fall with her amid the tangled
sheets and make fast, furious love to her. She seemed
to want the same thing as her fingers moved to the first
button of his fly and began to fumble to unfasten it.
He grabbed her hands, recognizing that she was a
woman accustomed to being in control and this time,
with him, he intended to be in control.

She looked up at him, her eyes hungry and her lips
slightly swollen and partly open as if to invite him to
another kiss. "Let me," he said as he dropped her
hands and instead reached for the button on her fly.

He'd expected an argument, but she surprised him
by standing perfectly still as he unfastened the top
button of her jeans. One by one he unbuttoned until
there was nothing more to unfasten.

When he'd finished she shimmied her jeans to the floor and stepped out of them. Her body was still hidden from his view by the length of her shirt. He reached for the bottom of her top, but she stepped back from him.

"The lamp," she said in a faint whisper.

"I want it on." He reached out and dragged a finger down the side of her face. She closed her eyes for a moment as if finding his touch excruciatingly intense.

"I don't want to fumble around in the dark with you," he said, his voice a husky rasp. "I want to look at your face while I'm touching you, I want to see your eyes when I make love to you."

She opened her eyes, inhaled a tremulous breath and pulled her T-shirt over her head. She dropped it to the floor and stood naked and proud in front of him.

The sight of her stole his breath away. Her hips were curvy and her stomach was flat. Her smallish breasts begged to be touched. To him she was stunning…absolutely perfect.

As he tore off his jeans, she crawled beneath the sheets of the bed and when he joined her there he pulled her into his arms for a full-contact body embrace.

She felt just as she had in his dreams, soft and hot, eager and beyond tempting. Their mouths met once again as his hands found the fullness of her breasts and cupped them.

As his thumbs stroked across her nipples she released a low, deep moan. He tore his mouth from hers and looked down at her, saw the darkened irises of her eyes, eyes filled with a hunger that torched through him.

He could have taken her then, buried himself inside her and taken her in frantic need. But he didn't. He had no idea how many lovers she'd had before, but he wanted to make love to her better than any other man ever had. He wanted her to remember her cowboy lover long after she left Cotter Creek and him behind.

With this thought in mind, he began to explore her body inch by delectable inch. He stroked and kissed as she clutched at him and moaned her pleasure. Each moan shot through him like a jolt of electricity, moving him closer to his point of no return.

He stoked her at her center, using his fingers to drive her mindless. She moaned his name, and he loved the sound of it on her lips. Her hips moved against him in frantic need and he increased the pressure of his touch.

It took only moments for her to stiffen and cry out, a soft mewling cry as she shuddered her release.

He could wait no longer. He leaned over and ripped open the drawer of his nightstand. His fingers trembled as he clasped one of the foil packets. Hurry, his brain screamed as he ripped it open and quickly rolled on the condom. Need drove him into her, and as he buried himself in her sweet, wet warmth he lost all sense of himself.

Together their hips moved in unison as his mouth once again found hers. Faster and faster they moved, their mouths no longer capable of clinging to each other while their bodies moved in raging need.

He felt her stiffening again, watched her eyelids flutter and her eyes roll back and then close and knew she had once again found her release.

It was all he needed to let himself go.

Moments later they remained in each other's arms, and for the first time Tanner recognized how utterly foolish they had been giving in to the desire that had been pulsating between them for the past couple of days.

"Anna." He rose on one elbow and gazed at her.

She reached up and laid a gentle hand on the side of his face. She looked at him as if she could see all that lay inside him. "You need to talk?"

Her soft touch, her knowing eyes and the invitation to share scared the hell out of him. In a matter of days she'd be gone, back to her superficial life of leisure.

No matter what they had just shared physically, he didn't intend to share anything with her emotionally. There was no point to baring his soul.

"No. What I really need is to sleep."

He hadn't realized how gruff he'd sounded until she jerked her hand away from him as if he'd slapped her. With one graceful movement she slid from the bed and stood. "Then I guess I'd better let you get some sleep."

With the dignity of a queen, she grabbed her jeans

and T-shirt, then slid out of his bedroom door and shut it behind her.

Tanner leaned his head back against the pillow and closed his eyes even though he knew sleep would be a long time coming. He'd hurt her by sending her away so abruptly, but the last thing he wanted to do was to snuggle beneath warm, sex-scented sheets and share the secrets of his heart.

Still her natural empathy got to him. If she really had been the spoiled young woman he believed she was, then she wouldn't have noticed or cared that Zack's words had bothered him. But apparently she had noticed and she did care.

He found his thoughts drifting away from Anna and to his brother. Zack's words had stung more deeply than he'd believed possible. He'd needed a brother, not a boss, that's what Zack had said.

Tanner had been trying to be a brother. He couldn't help it that his concern had been not only for Zack but for how Zack's actions might affect the company. The company was built for the benefit of his siblings. Tanner had worked hard to make the company successful enough that hopefully his siblings would never have to worry about money.

Zack was a hell of a bodyguard, a huge asset to Wild West Protective Services. Tanner couldn't imagine his brother not working for the agency. Zack belonged with the agency and Tanner knew that better than anyone. He'd just been trying to make Zack see that point.

He turned to his side as his thoughts once again returned to Anna. Anna, the spoiled, jet-setting princess. Anna, with gold in her hair and challenge sparkling her eyes. Anna, with her satiny skin and throaty sighs.

He hoped her father arrived tomorrow and would take her away from here, back to the life where she belonged.

Yes, this night had been a mistake and would have never happened had he not been feeling vulnerable. It was a mistake that wouldn't ever happen again.

Tanner West was the most aggravating man she'd ever known in her entire life. He was driven, arrogant and far more complex than she'd realized.

Last night he'd made exquisite love to her and there had been a moment when she'd felt him open to her not only with his body but with his heart and soul, as well. There had been a moment when he'd looked into her eyes and she'd seen the man beneath and he'd taken her breath away.

Unfortunately he'd ruined everything by shutting down and turning off, by throwing her to the curb before her heartbeat had even returned to a normal rhythm.

This morning had been no better. He'd been cranky and distant, pacing the floor in the great room and studiously ignoring her.

She felt a bit cranky herself. There was only so many times she could thumb through a copy of

*Ranch Living,* only so many times she could stare out the window and only so much silence she could handle.

It was just before noon when desperation drove her into Smokey's lair, the kitchen. "What do you want?" He looked about as inviting as the act of shoving a size-five shoe onto a size-seven foot.

"I want to know what it is about living in the middle of nowhere that makes everyone so darned crabby." She pulled out a stool and sat at the counter where Smokey was cutting up vegetables.

"Who's crabby?"

She eyed him through narrowed eyes. "Oh, I forgot, you're the epitome of cheerful," she said dryly.

A whisper of a twinkle lit Smokey's eyes. "I am what I am, and I don't pretend to put on airs."

"Is that what you think I do? Put on airs?" She propped her elbow on the counter and placed her chin in her hand.

A full grin pulled Smokey's worn features upward. "I think you were probably born with airs, but that's not your fault. That's just a circumstance of birth."

She frowned thoughtfully. "Then why do I get the feeling he blames me for my circumstance of birth?"

Smokey shrugged. "If Tanner's got a problem with you it's not because of your birth, but maybe because of the choices you've made in your life."

He resumed cutting up cucumbers. "That man is hard on people, but not half as hard as he is on himself. He stopped being a kid, stopped having fun the day his mama died."

"But he was just a little boy," she exclaimed.

"That he was, but that day he shed boyhood and became a man." Smokey set the cucumbers aside and reached for several large tomatoes. "He wasn't just a ten-year-old boy, he was the eldest of six younguns who were all confused and scared and wanting their mama. Red wasn't no good. He fell into a hole of booze and grief. I wasn't much better. Them kids didn't know me very well and it was Tanner who held them all together."

Anna watched for a moment as Smokey expertly sliced and diced the tomatoes, her thoughts embracing the little boy Tanner had been. Her heart cried for the boy who had become a man too soon, raised by life tragedy.

"Tanner doesn't know nothin' but work." Smokey continued speaking in the rough-hewn voice that was oddly appealing. "Since he was a teenager he's been determined to build something secure for his family. That business is all he thinks about, all he cares about."

He turned from the counter and went to the refrigerator. He grabbed several green peppers from the bin then returned to the cutting board and cast her a sly look. "I think a woman like you might be good for him."

"A woman like me?"

He sliced into one of the green peppers, the pungent scent filling the air. "You know, a woman who

knows how to have fun…maybe a little too much fun."
Again he gazed at her with that sly glance.

Anna had never in her life felt the need to apologize or to defend her lifestyle, but she did now. She had the strongest desire to not only apologize but to vow to herself that somehow, some way when this was all over she'd change her life.

"Maybe you're right. Maybe I've had a little too much fun in my life." She thought of the traveling, the clubbing, the frantic kind of fun she'd had. It certainly hadn't brought her anything close to happiness.

The phone rang and Smokey ignored it. It rang only once then apparently was answered by either Tanner or his father. Smokey continued cutting the peppers. "Nothing wrong with fun, but everyone needs a little work in their life, too. Something that makes them feel good about themselves. A man like Tanner would be good for you, too."

She wanted to snort in derision, to protest long and loudly, but deep inside she couldn't fool herself into thinking that Tanner meant nothing to her.

She didn't sleep with men who meant nothing. Men who meant nothing didn't have the potential to hurt her and she thought Tanner possessed that potential.

"It would take a better woman than me to bring a little fun to Tanner's life," she finally exclaimed.

"I don't know about that. I never thought I'd see the day that he'd be standing in front of my refrigerator sorting through things for a picnic."

"A picnic we never got to enjoy," she said wistfully.

"Maybe there will be another time for a picnic," Smokey said.

"Maybe," she agreed, although she doubted it. She was aware that her days here were definitely limited. At any moment her father could arrive and take her away from this ranch where she hadn't wanted to be and now almost hated to leave. She frowned thoughtfully. When had that happened? When had this place begun to feel like home?

The phone rang again. It was not an unusual occurrence. Most mornings the phone rang often as Tanner's agents checked in with him for the day.

"Is there anything I can do to help with lunch?" she asked.

Smokey's gray eyebrows danced upward. "You show a lot of potential, young lady. If you want, you can get the dishes out to set the table." He motioned toward one of the cabinets.

Potential. Nobody had ever told her she had potential before. Smokey's words warmed her as she took the plates out of the cabinet and carried them into the dining room.

There had never been any expectations for her. She was the sum of her frivolity, encouraged to be carefree and superficial and utterly empty inside.

She'd just returned to the kitchen to retrieve the silverware when Tanner came in, his features as grim as she'd ever seen them.

"Something's happened," he said.

"What?" The tension rolling off him forced her heart to beat faster. She was vaguely aware of Smokey setting down his knife, his grizzly brows pulled together.

"Linda Wilcox was found unconscious in an alley this morning." Tanner and Smokey exchanged a glance. "She'd been hit over the head with something and left there."

"That's horrible," she exclaimed. "Was she a friend of yours?"

"Just an acquaintance," Tanner said.

"Why did he call you?" Smokey asked.

"He thought I might be interested."

"He calling everyone in town or did he have a specific reason for thinking you might be especially interested?" Smokey asked.

Tanner's gaze held Anna's and she felt as if the pit of her stomach hit the floor. "He thought we'd be especially interested."

"Why?" The single word crawled from Anna's throat.

"Linda has blond hair, kind of loose around her shoulders like yours. Sheriff Ramsey thought it was interesting that she was wearing your clothes, Anna. The clothes you left at Betty's Boutique."

# Chapter 10

Tanner paced in front of the window, waiting for Jim Ramsey to arrive. Anna sat on the sofa, her face blanched of color as she watched him walk back and forth.

Over the years Tanner had worked on hundreds of assignments. He'd headed up protection for a rock star on a six-week tour, had guarded a priceless painting on display at a museum in Phoenix. He'd worked for politicians and businessmen, starlets and athletes, but he'd never had an assignment that worried him more than this one.

He couldn't get a handle on the bad guys, didn't understand them. Always before Tanner had relied on his instincts, but his instincts had been ominously silent on this particular assignment.

"It could just be some awful coincidence," Anna said tentatively, breaking in to his thoughts.

He stopped his pacing and turned to look at her once again. "Yeah, could be," he replied. But he didn't think so. There was a twist in his gut that made him fear it was something much worse than coincidence.

"Why is the sheriff coming to speak to us?" she asked, worry evident in her voice.

"I asked him to come out." Tanner tamped down his restless energy enough to sit next to her on the sofa. "I asked him to bring us the clothes Linda was wearing when she was attacked. I want to make sure they really are the ones you left at Betty's. Maybe she was wearing something similar and Betty got it wrong. If they are the clothes that belonged to you, then I want to go over them."

She frowned. "What do you mean, go over them? It was just a blouse and a long skirt. What's to go over?"

"I don't know. I just want to look at them." He needed to know if that skirt and blouse had somehow led to Linda's attack. He wasn't sure what he was looking for, but he wanted to see those articles of clothing.

Anna leaned into him, her warmth welcome despite his morning of regrets. "I hope Linda Wilcox was the victim of a random mugger. I hope she had a boyfriend who went crazy with jealousy. I hope anything explains what happened to her other than me being the cause of her pain."

He hadn't thought it possible that she would take some sort of personal responsibility for Linda's attack. He wrapped an arm around her shoulder and looked down into her troubled blue eyes. "Anna, you aren't responsible for what's happened. Whoever knocked Linda over the head is solely responsible for this."

"Yes, but if I hadn't come here...if I hadn't left those clothes at Betty's..."

He placed a finger against her soft, sweet lips. "If Betty hadn't resold them, if Linda hadn't bought them...if...if...if."

She grabbed his hand with both of hers and squeezed, her gaze vulnerable and unsure as it held his. Suddenly he felt like the biggest jerk on earth. He'd made love to her then had unceremoniously tossed her out of bed and had spent the morning subtly punishing her with his silence.

"Anna...about last night," he began, unsure what he intended to say but feeling as though he needed to say something.

"I wasn't exactly a gentleman and I apologize for being so brusque with you."

"Apology accepted," she said easily. She gazed at him with her clear, beautiful blue eyes and again he was surprised by the fact that she held no grudge.

"I just didn't want you to think that what happened…"

"Meant anything?" She raised one pale eyebrow. She offered him a faint smile. "The way I look at it we're both adults. There's been some kind of chemistry between us and last night we acted upon it. For as long as it lasted it was beautiful, but I wasn't expecting any hearts or flowers afterward, certainly not from a man like you. I'm just glad about one thing."

"What's that?"

Her dimples flashed. "At least you didn't tell me what to do or accuse me of breaking one of your rules."

His laughter surprised him, momentarily breaking the tension that had held him in its grip. The laughter felt good and he gazed at her almost gratefully. "I told you I didn't have any rules for lovemaking."

"Yes, but I wasn't sure I believed you."

Unfortunately the light moment between them lasted only a minute as the sound of gravel beneath car wheels drifted through the window.

He jumped up from the sofa and was at the front door as Jim Ramsey pulled his patrol car to a halt in the driveway. Once again the twist was in his gut as he watched the beefy man climb out of his car and head toward the porch.

Because it had been Jim Ramsey who had delivered the news of his mother's death, Tanner had never been able to completely separate Ramsey from his mother's murder. In his mind, the two were forever bound together in tragedy, even though Tanner knew it was irrational.

In Jim's hand he carried a brown bag that Tanner knew contained the clothes Linda Wilcox had been wearing before somebody slammed her over the head.

"Tanner." Jim greeted him with a grim smile. "You know I'm breaking about a hundred rules to bring you these clothes." He stepped through the door and nodded to Anna, then turned once again to Tanner. "You going to tell me what the hell is going on?"

Tanner hesitated a moment. Although he and Jim had always been civil to one another and there had been times in the past when Tanner had called on the sheriff to help him with a protection problem, Tanner had never felt any bond, no real connection to the man. He'd always felt that the sheriff helped not because he respected Tanner and the work they did, but merely because it was his job.

"Let me see what you've got and I'll tell you if anything is going on," he said. He gestured for the sheriff and Anna to follow him into the kitchen.

He didn't want to tell Ramsey any more than necessary. He still believed that Anna's safety depended on nobody knowing who she was.

He could tell Ramsey wasn't pleased with his answer, but the sheriff walked into the kitchen and set the bag on the table after giving a curt nod to Smokey.

"Where's your father?" he asked as he opened the bag.

"He drove into Oklahoma City this morning," Tanner replied. His father had left before dawn to see what he could find out about the murder of the woman Zack had been protecting.

Red wanted to talk to the authorities and to get the details of what had gone wrong. Tanner knew it was his father's attempt to find out something, anything, that would ease Zack's guilt and grief.

"What can you tell me about Linda's attack?" Tanner asked, aware of Anna moving closer to him as if needing him near as she heard the details.

"Mind if I sit?" Ramsey didn't wait for a reply, but pulled out a chair and eased down, the bag in front of him on the table. "Been a long day and it isn't even noon yet."

Anna sank into the chair across from him and Tanner wondered if it would have been better had she gone to her room and not been a part of any of this.

Sitting next to Ramsey, he reminded himself that she needed to be here. She needed to know what was going on. After all, it was her life, her safety they were concerned about.

"Early this morning Ted Miller went into the alley behind his feed store to empty some garbage cans. That's where he found Linda." Ramsey shook his head. "Like I told you on the phone, she'd been knocked pretty hard on the back of her head. She was unconscious when she was found, but she came to about an hour ago."

"Was she able to tell you who attacked her?" Tanner asked.

Jim frowned once again. "She doesn't know. She remembers going to Betty's and buying new clothes. She changed into them before she left the shop, then she went to the café for dinner. It was as she was walking home that somebody came up from behind and dragged her into the alley. It was dark, and she said whoever it was shined a flashlight in her face, cursed, then slammed her in the head and that's all she remembers."

"Any suspects?" Tanner was aware of Anna leaning forward, her eyes begging Ramsey to have a suspect in custody or at least somebody in mind.

"None." Ramsey's blunt features pulled together in a frown. "She's a nice young woman who doesn't seem to have an enemy in the world. No boyfriend in the picture at the moment, no old boyfriends that were threatening or seemed to be any kind of a problem. Why did you want me to bring her clothes?"

"I just want to look at them," Tanner said.

Ramsey's brown eyes held Tanner's gaze. "You got a reason you're willing to share?"

"I'll let you know if I find what I'm looking for."

Ramsey frowned, but he reluctantly reached his hand into the bag and withdrew the two articles of clothing. The first item he pulled out of the bag was a long navy skirt, the same one Anna had worn when she'd first come into Tanner's office, the same one she'd left at Betty's on the day they had bought her new clothing.

Tanner took the skirt and began to check every inch of it, feeling the fabric, staring at the detail of material and thread. He focused on finding something— anything—that would explain how it was possible that the rebels might have come to Cotter Creek and thought that Linda was the princess they sought.

"What are you looking for?" Anna asked.

"I'm not sure."

They were all silent as Tanner worked his fingers over every inch of the skirt. When he was finished he motioned for Jim to hand him the blouse.

The blouse was silk with large decorative buttons down the front and at each wrist. He was aware of the tense silence of the room as he worked the silk through his fingers, exploring the blouse inch by inch.

"Smokey, hand me a mallet, would you?" he asked when he was finished going over the material.

"What are you fixing to do?" Jim asked, a touch of worry in his voice.

"I'll show you." Tanner took the mallet, normally used to tenderize meat, and without warning smashed it against one of the buttons on the blouse.

"Tanner!" Anna exclaimed as the button was crushed into pieces. Jim said nothing and Tanner had a feeling the sheriff knew exactly what he was doing.

Systematically Tanner crushed every button down the front of the blouse, then moved to the two on the wrists. He found what he had suspected in the first wrist button and his pulse thundered in his veins.

"What's that?" Anna asked, staring at the tiny device that had been hidden inside the plump button.

Tanner held it up between his fingertips. "If I was to guess, I'd say this is some sort of tracking device. This is how they know you're here in Cotter Creek."

The afternoon took on a surreal quality for Anna. In the space of Tanner cracking open a button, everything had changed. She listened as he told Sheriff Ramsey her real identity and why she was here.

However, Tanner assured the sheriff things were under control and he didn't need Ramsey to do anything but keep his mouth shut about Anna's location. "It's a matter of life or death to the princess," he said.

After the sheriff left, Tanner, Smokey and Anna remained seated at the kitchen table as Tanner told Anna how everything had changed.

"Although they know you're in Cotter Creek, it's obvious by the attack on Linda that they aren't sure exactly where you are," he said.

"But it's just a matter of time," she said flatly.

He nodded, his eyes darkly hooded. "Unfortunately, we just ran out of time. If that tracking device was working when Jim arrived, then they will have tracked the blouse to this ranch. We need to make immediate adjustments."

"Like what?" There was no hint of the man who had made love to her the night before or the man who had laughed with her a little while ago. His green eyes were cold, calculating, and she felt his energy as if it were another human presence in the room.

"The first thing I'm going to do is triple the guards around the house. I want armed guards every ten feet around the perimeter. I'll also put some on the road coming up to the house. But the major difference is that you aren't going to be here."

Anna frowned. "But my father is expecting me to be here."

"You'll be here at the ranch, but you won't be here in this house."

She stared at him with wariness. "You aren't going to stick me in the stable, are you?" She'd hoped for a smile, but got none.

His jaw was tense, his lips a grim slash. "We'll move you after dark tonight. We'll move you to my place." He exchanged looks with Smokey. "Hopefully the guard presence on this house will work as a diversion. The rebels will assume you're in here because of the visibility of the guards."

He looked back at Anna. "The only way the rebels will know that you aren't in this house is if they come through my men." His jaw clenched tighter. "And that's not going to happen."

Anna fought against a shiver. For the past three days she'd felt utterly safe here at the ranch. She'd believed the rebels had had no idea where she was, no idea how to find her, but now she knew simply by looking into Tanner's bottle-green eyes that danger was near, far too near.

Tanner turned his attention to her once again. "Why don't you go pack your things? Smokey will find you a suitcase to use, and while you're doing that I'm going to make some phone calls."

The afternoon and evening alternated between flying too fast for thoughts and creeping by with excruciating slowness. Anna packed her things into a small suitcase, then returned to the living room to sit on the sofa and wait until dinner.

She was aware of men arriving and departing from Tanner's study, hard-looking men with rifles in hand and a grim purpose in their steps. Although they were all dressed like cowpokes, she knew they were much more than that. They were the men who would be on guard duty here at the house.

It was just after a quiet supper that Red returned from the city. Tanner took his father into the study and Anna knew he was filling Red in on what had occurred and the new plans Tanner had made.

As the two men remained locked in the study, Anna helped Smokey clear the table. "You doing okay?" Smokey asked.

"I'm fine. Why?"

"A princess helping to clear a table doesn't happen every day around here."

She flashed him a quick smile. "If you're nice to me, this princess might even help wash and dry the dishes." She grabbed the plates off the table and followed Smokey into the kitchen. "I kind of like doing this kind of work," she said. "Nobody has ever let me before."

"Any housework you want to do around here, you knock yourself out, ain't nobody going to tell you to stop," Smokey replied. She laughed and decided that Smokey had a certain charm all his own.

They finished clearing the table, then stood side by side at the sink as Smokey washed and Anna dried. "Have you ever been married, Smokey?"

"Nah, never could find a woman who'd put up with me for more than a minute or two. Besides, for a lot of years I was needed here. Still am, far as I know."

"Did you know Tanner's mother?" she asked.

"Sure. Everyone knew Elizabeth West." Smokey squirted more dish soap into the sinkful of water.

"What was she like?"

"She was a fine woman, always cooking pies for sick neighbors, taking baskets of goodies to the kids at the hospital. To look at her, you'd have thought she was one of those Hollywood types. She was Red's first protection assignment."

"Really?"

Smokey grabbed a dirty plate and sank it in the water. "She was making her second movie and Red was working on the set as a stunt man. Seems some wacko had taken a shine to her, was stalking her and scaring her. Red offered to work as her bodyguard and the rest, as they say, is history."

Anna found the information interesting. She'd just assumed that Tanner's mother had been born and raised in the small town with dreams no bigger than a house of her own and kids.

It intrigued her to know that Elizabeth had been a Hollywood starlet. She'd obviously had big dreams and, if she was making her second movie, a certain measure of success. But she'd left all that behind to marry Red and to move to Cotter Creek and have a house full of children.

"She didn't mind moving out here?"

"According to what Red told me, she would have moved to Alaska and lived in an igloo if it meant being with him and having her family. Those were her priorities, not the tinsel and glitz of Hollywood."

Elizabeth West had chosen the beauty of sunrises over the sparkle of jewels, the sound of childrens' laughter instead of the raucous music of a club. She'd chosen the love of one good man over the adulation of thousands of fans. She'd obviously been not only beautiful, but smart, as well.

She and Smokey had just finished with the dishes when Tanner came into the kitchen, his features still set in the grim lines that had taken up residence for most of the afternoon.

"We're all set," he said as he sank onto a chair. "I've got all the men I need. Now all we do is wait until dark, then we move."

She dried her hands on the dish towel, then joined him at the table. She wanted to touch him, to place her hand on his cheek, to lean her head against his chest to hear his heartbeat.

But she did none of these things. He looked forbidding, his features drawn tight, his eyes darker than she'd ever seen them. "I've got some questions for you," he said. "Tell me exactly what happened on the night of the coup in Niflheim."

"What do you mean?" she asked.

"You told me that you were awakened and hustled away from the palace. Who woke you up? Who picked out the clothes you put on? Who had access to your clothing?" The questions came from him fast and sharp.

She frowned, trying to remember that night when she'd been awakened with the news that her life was in danger. Had it been only a little more than a week ago? It felt as if at least two lifetimes had passed since that night.

"I was awakened by one of my bodyguards. He burst into my room and told me that the palace was about to be lost to the rebels and my father and I had to leave immediately. Astrid, my personal assistant and maid, came in right behind him. She got my clothes for me. She packed a couple of suitcases for me."

The sense of betrayal that swept through her cut deep and brought a small gasp to her lips. Tanner's eyes softened slightly as he continued to gaze at her. "You didn't pick out your own clothes? She got them for you?"

She nodded. "Astrid." The name fell from her lips softly as her heart constricted tightly. "I thought she was my friend. She was the one person in my life I thought I could trust. I thought she cared about me, but she betrayed me. She had to have known about the tracking devices, had to have known what clothes to pack."

"It's possible somebody else could have been responsible." he said. "Who knows how many of those little technical bugs might have been in your suitcases."

Again a weary sense of betrayal filled her heart. Political intrigue, betrayal by friends…why would anyone want to be a king or a princess? Why would anyone want to live a life of never knowing whom to trust, whom to depend on?

At least here and now, she knew she could trust Tanner. She knew she could depend on him no matter what happened. She leaned back in her seat and sighed. "Thank you, Tanner, for everything you're doing for me," she said.

His brooding eyes flashed with a touch of impatience. "I'm just doing my job."

His job. Yes, that's what she needed to remember.

Even though they had made love, she was nothing more than a job to him, an important job that if successful would earn Wild West Protective Services a sterling reputation and more success than Tanner could dream of.

Before anyone could say anything else the back door opened and Zack walked in. He nodded at Anna, then looked at his brother. "Heard there might be some trouble," he said.

Tanner stood. "Could be."

"Know what you're up against?"

"Don't have a clue," Tanner replied, his frustration evident in his voice.

"I'll stand guard duty. I'm not coming back to work for the agency, but I'll help protect what is ours," Zack said.

It was at that moment that Anna truly realized what was at risk. Her presence was threatening not only the lives of each and every person on the ranch, but the very ranch itself. The rebels could set off a bomb, toss a grenade or set a fire to the West family home.

These people were risking everything for her, and in that instant Anna realized she was precariously close to falling in love with Tanner West.

## Chapter 11

Darkness didn't steal in gently, but seemed to drop like a blanket across the earth. Clouds obscured even the faintest moonlight, which suited Tanner's needs very well.

The darkness was their friend when it came to moving Anna from the big house into his home. Although the distance between the two structures wasn't that great, it was a distance where they would be vulnerable to a sniper's intent.

Finding the bug in the button of Anna's blouse had galvanized and recentered him. He was angry with himself for growing lax, for succumbing to Anna's charm and momentarily forgetting exactly what was at stake.

It was not only the reputation of the agency at risk if something should go wrong, but Anna's very life. Failure definitely wasn't an option.

It was just before ten when he and Anna prepared to leave the house. The guards were on duty, silent sentries watching for danger.

He turned to Anna, saw the slight tremble to her lips, the paleness of her skin. "It's going to be fine," he said. "All you need to do when we step outside is to hold my hand and keep quiet. You ready?"

She nodded and he grabbed her hand in one of his, her suitcase in the other. Together they walked out the front door then stepped off the porch and headed in the direction of his house. Her hand was cool in his and trembled slightly. The feel of it, so soft and yielding, swelled in his chest.

He told himself the overwhelming surge of emotion was because of the importance of the job he was doing. He tried to convince himself that his emotions had nothing to do with the softness of her skin or the sound of her laughter. It had nothing to do with the stubbornness he found oddly charming or the fact that over the past couple of days she'd even managed to win Smokey's affection.

When he'd walked into the kitchen just after supper and seen her standing at the sink helping Smokey finish up the dinner dishes, he'd been shocked. The princess was transforming right before his eyes, and it was a transformation that made both a feeling of satisfaction and discomfort sweep through him.

He focused on the here and now, his eyes quickly adjusting to the darkness. They didn't run, but walked at a fast pace, the light he'd left on in his living room shining like a beacon in the darkness that surrounded them. He knew the trees and brush around his place would hide the additional men he'd called on and some of Cotter Creek's finest.

True to his instructions, she said not a word, made not a sound, and he didn't breathe until they were safely inside the house and behind a closed, locked door.

He watched her as she looked around the living room with interest. "It's nice," she said.

"No, it isn't." He set her suitcase down and gazed at the room as if seeing it for the very first time. A couch, a chair, a coffee table and a television were the sum of the interior decorating.

It was a room without personality, without warmth or life. It was a perfect reflection of the man who lived here.

He frowned. Where had that thought come from? "I'll put you in the master bed and I'll sleep on the floor in there," he explained. "Even though there are three bedrooms, two of them are empty. I haven't gotten around to doing anything with them."

"I don't want to take your bed. I'll be happy to sleep on the floor," she replied.

"I'm on the floor," he said firmly. "That keeps me between you and the front door." He walked around the room, twisting the blinds closed on every window as she sank onto the sofa.

He hoped he hadn't made an error in not taking her off the ranch altogether, but this was familiar territory and there was a certain comfort, a certain security in knowing his surroundings.

He just hoped his little ploy worked and they would assume by the visible guards that she was in the main house. He had every confidence that the men guarding the main house could handle whatever might come their way. And if by chance their ploy didn't work, this house was guarded, as well.

Anna curled her feet beneath her, looking as if she belonged on the navy sofa. "So what happens now?"

"We wait. We see who shows up first, your father or the rebels. Want some coffee?"

"That sounds good. I'm certainly too wound up to go to bed."

He walked into the kitchen, twisted the blinds tightly closed, then set about making a pot of coffee. He had a feeling this was going to be the most difficult part of the assignment, being alone with her in his house for an undetermined amount of time.

Moments later he carried two cups of coffee into the living room and joined her on the sofa, making sure he kept as much distance as possible between them.

"Thank you," she said as he handed her one of the

cups. For a few minutes they sat in silence and sipped their coffees. Tanner tried to ignore the scent of her, a scent that had become as familiar as the smell of sunshine on the Oklahoma ground.

"I'll bet you'll be glad when this is all over," he said, finally breaking the silence between them.

She took another sip of the coffee and eyed him thoughtfully over the rim of the cup. "I'll be glad when the danger has passed."

"Can't wait to get back to shopping and yachting and doing all the things that princesses do?" He expected a sharp retort from her, but instead she shrugged her shoulders, looking small and vulnerable.

"I'm sure my father loves me in his own way," she said, and looked down into her cup. "But he's always dismissed me, had little expectations of me, and that's what I lived up to." She looked at Tanner once again. "And I've always had this terrible loneliness inside me, a loneliness I thought I could still by shopping and traveling and partying."

She uncurled her legs from beneath her and set her cup on the glass-topped coffee table. "I've had a lot of time to think in the past couple of days and whatever the future holds, I intend to make different choices concerning my lifestyle."

Tanner didn't want to hear this. He didn't want to think of her suffering loneliness, perhaps the same kind of loneliness that haunted him at odd hours of the day and night.

He also strangely didn't want to hear about her decision to make better choices in her life. He was afraid she might become in his mind a woman he could fall in love with.

He stood and picked up her cup from the coffee table. "It's getting late. We should get settled in for the night."

She frowned and didn't move from the sofa. "Do you realize almost every night I've been here you've sent me to bed like a child?"

"There's nothing wrong with structure in your life."

"Structure…rules…that's all you seem to know. I was trying to talk to you, to tell you how things have changed for me since I've been here. I was trying to share with you and all you can do is stick to the rules." Her chin rose in a touch of defiance. "Maybe I'm not sleepy yet."

He wasn't sure if she was trying to pick a fight or just being difficult in general. But the last thing he wanted was to sit around and listen to her talk about her transformation from spoiled willful princess to something else.

"I don't give a damn if you dance around in the bedroom until dawn. I don't care if you sit and make lists of all the things you're going to do when you leave here until the sun comes up. But right now I'm tired and it's time to go to bed."

He hadn't realized when it had happened, had no idea that somewhere in the course of the past few days he had gained the power to hurt her, but he had and hurt now shone from her eyes. It was there for just a moment, then masked beneath a facade of coolness as she stood.

"I apologize. I don't want to keep you from getting a good night's sleep. If you'll just show me to my room, I won't bother you for the rest of the night."

He picked up her suitcase and carried it into the master bedroom, trying not to feel guilty about shutting her down, shutting her up. He went to the two windows in the room and checked to make sure they were locked, then closed the blinds.

This room held no more personality than the living room. The bed was neatly made with a brown spread and a small lamp set on the nightstand. The dresser, a rich cherrywood, held nothing on its gleaming top. For some reason, the sight of the room that had been his for the past three years depressed him.

He placed her suitcase on the bed, then turned to look at her. "There's some new rules while we're here."

"What?" She sat on the bed and eyed him with a touch of weariness.

"First of all, we sleep with the bedroom door open. I need to be able to hear if anyone tries to break through any of the windows or if anything threatens us."

She nodded, her eyes more somber than they'd been moments before. "Second," he continued, "you don't go near the windows. Don't even open them a sliver to look outside. And last of all, no more sleeping in the nude. If anything happens in the middle of the night, we might have to make a run for it. I don't want you naked and running around for everyone to see."

"Is that it?"

"For now."

She reached behind her, grabbed one of the bed pillows and threw it to him with more force than necessary. "Fine, then get out of my bedroom long enough for me to get ready for bed."

He carried the pillow back into the living room and tossed it on the sofa, but sleep was the last thing on his mind. He'd needed to shut her down, had been afraid of what she might confess in her monologue of sharing her innermost thoughts. There was no telling what might come out of her mouth and he didn't want things more complicated than they already were.

As he walked around the interior of the house, double-checking that all the windows in each room were locked, he thought of his brother, Zack.

He had no idea exactly what had happened between Zack and his client in the three months that Zack had been on duty, but he'd seen the result. Zack had returned home a broken man because he'd allowed himself to get too close, to get emotionally involved.

Tanner absolutely refused to make the same mistake with Anna. No matter what happened, she wasn't meant for him. She was a princess, and despite her earlier words she would go back to being a princess once this was all over. One way or another, she would be out of his life, and he refused to put himself in a position to mourn her loss.

For three days they had been in his house, and the three days had been filled with stress as intense awareness of one another and a simmering tension grew by the moment.

Each night she slept in sheets that smelled of him, that clean male scent with a touch of the cologne he always wore. She'd burrow her head in the pillow and wonder why she had fallen in love with him. She fell asleep each night to the sound of him breathing as he lay on a bedroll on the floor. She suspected if he slept at all it was only briefly.

Despite the fact that he was bossy and a workaholic, in spite of the fact that he was reluctant to share meaningful pieces of himself, she loved him as she'd never loved a man before.

She wasn't sure when exactly she'd fallen in love with him, had no idea if there had been a single defining moment—she only knew what was in her heart.

There were moments when she felt his gaze on her, when she felt a connection with him that stole her breath away. There were moments when she saw a small smile begin to curve the corners of his mouth and she felt as if she'd been gifted with the riches of the world.

She loved the fact that he had worked so hard on behalf of his family, that his values were good even if he did need some balance.

She wanted him. She wanted him to sweep her up into his arms and make love to her through the long, lonely night. She wanted to feel his heartbeat against hers, to taste the heat of his kisses, to feel his big, strong hands against her skin.

But she had her pride and he had shown no indication, other than that whisper of hunger she occasionally saw flashing in his eyes, that he wanted a repeat of what they'd shared before.

While he'd spent his time pacing and brooding, she'd spent much of her time seated at the kitchen table playing hand after hand of solitaire with a deck of cards he'd found in one of the drawers.

It was now after dinner and Anna was once again at the kitchen table, the deck of cards in front of her. Tanner sat on the sofa, tension radiating from him to fill all the spaces of the house.

"I'm sick of solitaire," she announced. "Why don't you come over here and play a little poker with me?"

He raised a dark eyebrow. "Don't you realize all us cowboys are champions when it comes to poker playing?"

She grinned. "I'll bet you haven't played against a princess before."

She watched as he pulled himself up from the sofa and ambled toward the table, a lazy smile curving his lips. It was the first hint of a smile she'd seen from him since they'd come to his house and warmth cascaded through her at the sight.

He sat in the chair opposite hers and reached for the cards. Those wicked green eyes of his splashed her with heat. "So what are the stakes?"

Her heart beat a little faster. "Let's make it really interesting. How about some strip poker?" His eyebrows shot up and she saw the protest forming on his lips. Before he could voice it, she added, "What's wrong, Tanner? Afraid you'll lose?"

His eyes flashed with challenge and he reached for the deck of cards. She jumped up from the table. "Before we start, I need to do something. I'll be right back."

She went into her bedroom where she pulled on an extra T-shirt, two more socks and as a final thought stuck her crown on top of her head. There was no way she intended to be the first one naked.

When she returned to the table he grinned in obvious amusement. "Feeling a bit insecure, are we?"

She returned his grin, grateful for the break in the tension and stress. "Just hedging my bets." She grabbed the cards from him. "Five card stud, deuces wild. Ready to play?"

"Just a minute." He got up from the table and grabbed his cowboy hat and plopped it on his head.

"Just hedging my bets," he said as he sat once again. His eyes glittered with challenge. "Deal 'em, partner."

Within minutes she realized he was a tough adversary. She lost the first two hands, her extra socks. He lost the next and removed his hat, tossing it to the floor next to the table.

Back and forth they went for the next hour until she was down to her T-shirt and jeans. Her crown rested across the top of Tanner's boots, which sat just beside the table. He was shirtless and holding his cards close to his chest.

She had a pair of aces and a heart full of desire. She felt as if each hand they'd played had been a form of foreplay and her knees were weak with wanting him.

She knew he wanted her, too. She felt his desire radiating from him, saw it shining in his eyes. But he made no move to act on it. His eyes remained dark and he'd gotten more and more quiet as the game had gone on and articles of clothing had piled up.

"I'll see you," he said. "Read 'em and weep." He laid down his cards, showing a pair of queens.

Her aces beat his queens, but in the instant before she showed her hand, her mind raced. She wanted to make love with him again, but it was obvious he didn't intend to make any move to get her back into bed.

If she lost the hand, she'd literally lose her shirt. Would that be enough to make him lose control and shove him over the edge? Or was she imagining his desire for her because she wanted him so badly.

"You got me," she replied, and quickly added her cards to the discard pile. She stood and grabbed the bottom of her T-shirt, intent on pulling it over her head.

He jumped up from the table and grabbed her hands, halting her movement. "That's enough," he said. "We stop the game right now."

He stood so close to him she could see the tiny gold flecks in his green eyes, could feel the heat radiating off him as he held her hands tightly.

"I'm not playing a game anymore," she replied softly.

For a long moment they stood mere inches from each other, gazes locked as her heartbeat raced. His hands were hot on hers, as if he was consumed with fever.

With a muttered curse he pulled her to him, tangled his hands in her hair and took her mouth in a kiss that nearly buckled her knees.

The desire she'd thought she'd seen in his eyes was there in his kiss, in the way his hands gripped her hair, then slid down her back, pressing her close…closer against him.

It was silly, but she felt like crying as her love for him welled up and swelled in her chest. It wasn't just the fact that she loved the taste of his mouth or the way his hard body felt against hers. It wasn't merely that his touch electrified her.

When he was near, she didn't feel the loneliness that had always plagued her. She loved that he expected her to be a better woman than what she'd been. She loved him and she knew nothing in her life would ever be the same because of her love for him.

His mouth slid from hers and went to the hollow of her throat as his hands gripped her buttocks and pulled her more firmly against him.

She could feel his arousal and her ability to think edged away as she allowed herself to be overtaken by sheer physical pleasure.

"You make me crazy," he murmured against her ear. "You make me crazy with wanting you."

His words enflamed her.

"I'm crazy with wanting you," she gasped. "I haven't been able to think of anything else but being with you again."

His mouth claimed hers once again, making conversation impossible. Their tongues battled, dancing together in erotic play.

She wasn't sure how, didn't really remember walking the distance to the bedroom, but suddenly they were there, tearing off their clothes, then falling onto the bed and into each other's arms.

The urgency that had gripped him in the kitchen seemed to ebb as he began to stroke her skin. The darkness in the room made it impossible for her to see his face clearly, but she didn't need to see him.

She *saw* him through his touch as his hands cupped

her breasts and one of his legs rubbed against hers. She *saw* him in the kisses that scalded her lips with the fever of desire. She *saw* him in her soul, the man who held not just her safety in his hands, but her heart.

This time she helped him put on protection, loving the way he moaned at her intimate touch. When she was finished, his mouth moved down her throat, across her collarbone and to one of her nipples. She tangled her hands in his hair as he licked and teased the rigid peak. Shivers of delight worked up her spine at each touch of his mouth.

She felt fragile, as if every bone in her body had become soft and yielding. As his mouth moved from the underside of her breast down the flat of her abdomen, every nerve in her body sizzled with a growing tension that threatened to snap her in two.

His hands preceded his mouth, caressing her stomach, across her hips, then touching her softly at her center. She moaned his name with pleasure and thrust her hips upward to meet his intimate touch.

His ragged breathing filled the room along with her moans of pleasure as he stroked her and the tension inside her grew to unimaginable proportion.

Higher and higher he took her until there was nothing but his touch and her response. When she could go no higher, she went over the edge and crashed, shattering into a million pieces as she cried his name over and over again.

It was then, while she was weak and gasping, that

he moved back up her body and entered her. She wrapped her arms around his broad back and held him tight, wishing she could keep him this close to her forever.

She could feel his heartbeat thundering against hers as he remained unmoving for a long moment. His hands touched her on the sides of her face in a caress of infinite tenderness. The gesture brought tears to her eyes.

He filled up her body, but no more so than he filled up her heart. As he moved his hips against hers, stroking deep and slow, once again he swept her up to a dizzying height of pleasure.

"Anna," he whispered just before his lips claimed hers.

Her heart cried his name in return and then she was lost, beyond words, beyond thought, as he drove into her, bringing her to climax once again. He stiffened and moaned as he reached the pinnacle of his pleasure.

Moments later they remained tangled together amid the navy sheets, waiting for heartbeats to slow, for pulses to return to a more normal rate.

The tears that had filled her eyes earlier once again threatened. They were the physical expression of the emotions that burned inside her. Tears of joy. Tears of love.

He rolled her to her side and with one hand he stroked her hair. It seemed that she had been drifting all her life, seeking something…seeking someone.

She had degrees she hadn't used, skills and talents that had been thrown away by a life wasted in running away from herself.

In the brief time she'd been with Tanner and his family, she'd seen a different kind of life, one filled with love and respect, of work and self-fulfillment.

She realized she wanted to be a woman Tanner could respect, but more important she wanted to be a woman she could respect.

She looked at him, his features barely discernible in the near darkness of the room. There had been many times when she'd wondered what people did to fill the silences of the nights.

As she listened to the sound of Tanner's deep, even breathing, as she thought of the sweet words he'd murmured to her while he'd made love to her, she knew.

There was no silence for the people in Cotter Creek who spent their nights listening to their loved ones, comforted by the nearly inaudible sounds of hearts beating and love flourishing.

"You okay?" he asked, his voice a deep, soft whisper.

"I'm better than okay." Surely he loved her. Surely he couldn't make love to her as he did and not be in love with her. He couldn't look at her the way he did and not love her. "I've made some decisions."

He propped himself up on one elbow. "Decisions?"

"No matter what happens with my father in Niflheim, I'm not returning." The moment the words were

spoken out loud she knew the rightness of her decision. "There's nothing for me there. There never has
been anything there for me."

"So what will you do?" The questions seemed hesitant, as if he wasn't sure he wanted the answer.

"Arrange for citizenship, then maybe teach. I could
teach a foreign language or economics. I think I'd like
that...working with kids."

"Are you sure now is the best time to make life-
changing decisions?" he asked. "I mean, you've been
under a tremendous amount of stress and now might
not be the best time to make those kinds of decisions."

"When is a good time?" she countered. She wished
she could see his facial features better. "I've been un-
happy for a long time. This week here has given me time
to assess things, to figure out that going back to the
same kind of lifestyle isn't going to make me happy."

His finger smoothed across her lips, the gesture as
intimate as anything she had ever experienced. "You
deserve happiness, Anna."

She held her breath, hoping...praying he would
say something, anything that would indicate he hoped
she'd spend her life with him.

He had to love her. He had to, because she couldn't
imagine what she'd do if he didn't. *Tell him,* a little
voice whispered inside her. *Tell him how you feel.*

Her heart pounded as the words formed on her lips.
She had never wanted anything as much as she wanted
Tanner's respect, his love.

"I love you, Tanner." The words that had beat in her heart spilled from her lips and she knew that by speaking them out loud she had crossed a line and couldn't go back.

# *Chapter 12*

"I love you, Tanner."

It wasn't just the words that sent a weighty dread through him, but the sweet yearning, the naked emotion that was in her voice as she'd spoken them.

This wasn't supposed to happen. She wasn't supposed to fall in love with him. Those four words that she'd spoken were words he'd never expected to hear from her, hadn't wanted to hear from her.

A mistake. He'd made mistake after mistake where she was concerned and now he had the difficult task of trying to straighten out the mess and it was the worst kind of mess, one of sheer, naked emotions.

He'd rather wrestle with a gunman or face a psycho with a knife than do what he had to do now. He'd rather cut off his right arm than see the hurt he knew was about to steal over her features.

"Anna," he began, and sat up, needing to get some distance from her. "You might think you're in love with me, but I'm sure you're mistaking love for other feelings."

She leaned over and turned on the lamp on the nightstand. He tried not to notice how beautiful she looked with her hair in disarray and her lips slightly swollen from his kisses. She looked soft and sexy, except for her eyes, which glittered with familiar challenge.

"So you know what's in my heart and you think I must be mistaken?" Without warning, she hit him in the chest with her fist. "You are the most irritating, aggravating man I've ever known. You are so arrogant you think you know what I'm thinking, what I'm feeling, and you don't."

"Whoa." He caught her fist before she could hit him again, then scrambled from the bed and grabbed his jeans from the floor.

As he pulled them on, he was aware of her staring at him and knew she was waiting for some sort of a response. But for a moment he couldn't speak around the lump that had risen in his throat.

He raked a hand through his hair, wondering how on earth he'd allowed things to get so out of control. He'd never had this problem before with any of his assignments, and he'd had plenty of assignments in the past where he'd worked with pretty women. For God's sake, he was supposed to be on twenty-four-hour watch. What had he been thinking? That he'd find the rebels in the sheets on the bed? She should be just like all the other jobs he'd worked, but she wasn't.

Anna was different. She'd been different from the moment she'd come through his office door. She challenged him, excited him in a way nobody had ever done before. She made him laugh and somehow made him feel more vulnerable than he'd ever felt in his life.

"Anna, I'm sure whatever you think you feel for me is all tied up with the uncertainty in your life right now, the fear of being hunted, our forced proximity to each other and maybe more than a little bit of boredom."

Her eyes narrowed. "You think I'm in love with you because I'm bored? That's a horrible thing to say."

He grimaced. "I think it's a combination of things that have you mistaken."

"I know you think I'm worthless, a piece of fluff who has never done anything productive in her life." Her voice trembled with the depth of her emotion. "And in some ways you're right. I have been spoiled, I am willful, but that doesn't mean I don't know what's in my heart. I love you, Tanner West, and that's something you can't be in control of. It's my feelings, my emotions, and you can't change them no matter how much you might want to."

Why was this so hard? he wondered. Why did his

heart feel so heavy, so utterly dead? Zack had made him feel bad, but this was worse…far worse. It seemed so wrong, to break her heart even while the scent of her still lingered on his skin, in his pores.

"I'm sorry if I led you on," he said softly, "if I made you think there was something more than a strong physical desire between us."

He grabbed his gun from the dresser where he'd placed it as they'd entered the room, then left the bedroom, needing space from her luminous, slightly accusing eyes, needing distance from the scent of her, the very sight of her.

But she gave him no distance. As he shoved the gun into the waistband of his jeans, she appeared in the bedroom doorway, once again dressed in her jeans and the light blue T-shirt that did dazzling things to her eyes.

He'd never seen her look so vulnerable. There was no hint of the willful princess now, no touch of haughty disdain. There was only a woman with all her emotions naked and bared for him to see.

"I know you feel something more for me than just physical desire," she said. "I've seen it in your eyes. I've seen tenderness…caring. You can pretend this has been just a job to you, but I think it's been something more. You can pretend you don't care about me at all, but I know differently." She took several steps toward him.

"Anna, you've only known me for a week. I know

it seems longer, but it's only been a short period of time. Love doesn't happen that fast." He fought the impulse to step back from her.

Her eyes flashed once again, this time with a touch of annoyance. "Really? Then you tell me, Tanner, how long does it take to fall in love? What are your rules when it comes to matters of the heart?"

"There are no rules…"

"Exactly."

He sucked in a deep breath, wishing he were anywhere but in this room with her, in this room breaking her heart into pieces. "Anna, you're a princess. I'm a cowboy. We're from two different worlds." He tried to reason with her.

"You know what I think? I think you're a cowboy with fences around your heart and if you'd just let them fall like I've done with the walls around mine then you'd see what you really feel for me."

"Please, don't make this difficult." Instantly he knew they were the wrong words to say.

Her back stiffened. "Don't worry, Tanner. I won't play the poor, pitiful wronged woman and make things uncomfortable for you. I just want you to understand one thing. I love you and I would have made a good partner for you."

God, he wanted her to stop. He didn't want to hear any more. Her words were killing him inch by inch, but he felt the least he could do for her was to allow her to get it all out. He'd messed up big-time with her and he owed her to at least listen to her.

Tears shone in her eyes as she held his gaze. "It might have taken me time to completely understand your way of life, but I've always been a quick study. And I'll tell you this, I would have brought you laughter and passion."

She strode across the room and grabbed her crown from where it lay on the top of his boots. "I would have given you a daughter who would have worn this when she played dress-up and a son who could have one day filled your boots."

She tossed the crown onto the sofa, tears now running down her cheeks. "I've spent most of my life running away from the loneliness that plagued me, jetting off here and there, shopping until I wanted to be sick because I didn't want to take a look at who I was and where I was going. Where are you going, Tanner? What are you running away from with your workaholic lifestyle? With your need to never get personally involved with anyone?"

"Enough," he exclaimed. He didn't want to hear any more. He didn't want to hear the hurt in her voice, feel the strange gnawing pain that tore through his gut.

Again he raked his hand through his hair and averted his gaze from her. "Look, I made a mistake. I should have never indulged in my desire for you. I should have maintained professional integrity and never allowed this to happen."

It wasn't so much a shadow as a slight displacement of light outside the window that caught his attention. Instantly a surge of adrenaline seared through him as he reached up and grabbed the gun from his waistband.

"What are you going to do? Shoot me if I don't shut up?" she asked.

"I think there's somebody outside," he said in a deceptively calm, steady voice. "I want you to go to the bathroom, keep the light turned off and lock yourself inside. Do it now, Anna. No questions. Just do it and don't open the door again until you hear me...no matter what."

Already he was mentally far away from her and this room; focused instead on the knowledge that he was relatively certain there was somebody lurking just outside his house. None of his men would be walking so close to the house.

To his eternal gratefulness, she must have realized he was serious and wasn't just trying to change the subject. She didn't argue with him, but instead turned and hurried toward the bathroom.

Only when he heard the click of the lock did he quickly move through the house, turning off lights to even the odds with the darkness outside.

In each room after turning off the lights he crept to the windows and peeked through the slats of the blinds to see what might be out there. The half moon sent down just enough light to illuminate the landscape in ghostly hues.

There was nobody in the front of the house that he could see and he wondered if perhaps he had just imagined a presence. Had his mind conjured up a diversion from the painful conversation with Anna?

He got his answer when he peered through the windows of the master bedroom. There he saw the dark silhouette of a man running across the yard.

He quickly moved to the bedroom window on the east side of the house. Another tall, burly silhouette moved nearer the house.

At least two men. And they definitely weren't his men. If there were just two, he could take them. But he had no idea how many might be out there. Where were his men? Where were the cops?

While he had made love to Anna, a whole damn army could have surrounded the house. Dammit, another mistake he hoped he didn't have to pay for.

He grabbed his cell phone and punched in the number for the main house Smokey answered. "Something's going down," he said.

"Got it," Smokey replied, then clicked off. Tanner hung up as well, knowing that backup would be on the way. He still had no idea where the guards were that had been assigned on his place.

Just for his own information, he picked up the regular phone receiver.

Silence.

No dial tone.

Nothing. He wasn't surprised, but his heart still

pounded an unsteady rhythm. An attack was imminent. He knew it by the shadows moving around the
house, the dead phone line and the instincts that now
screamed of danger.

There was no way he intended to be in a defensive
position, not knowing what had happened to the half-
dozen men who were supposed to be stationed around
the house. He grabbed a knife and a roll of duct tape
and moved to the front door.

With grim intent he eased open the front door,
looked outside, then locked and closed the door behind
him and slid into the deepest shadows of the night.

For a moment he remained perfectly still, listening
for sounds of movement, the crackle of branches, the
whisper of footsteps against the grass. Before he
moved he needed to make sure there was nobody
nearby. He also hoped to hell that his own men didn't
put a bullet through his brain by accident.

The house was surrounded by trees on three sides,
and he knew if he could get into the cover of the trees
he could get a better idea of how many men lurked
around the perimeter of the house.

The immediate problem was getting to the cover of
the trees. Between the house and the tree line there was
about fifty yards where he would be visible and
vulnerable should he be seen.

His heartbeat had slowed the moment he'd stepped
outside. A calm, coolness swept through him, a feeling that was familiar and comforting.

Control. It was absolutely imperative that he maintain control and not allow any emotion to cloud his mind. Emotion got men killed.

He looked left, then right, his eyes adjusting to the near darkness of the night. He saw nothing, heard nobody, and with the stealth of a thief he crouched and moved fast toward the cover of the trees.

The grass was cool against his bare feet and he wished he'd taken a moment to pull on his boots. He hoped he didn't step on anything that would hobble him.

As he ran he tensed, as if expecting a warning shout from one rebel to another, or worse, a bullet in his back. He didn't take a breath until he'd reached the trees and leaned with his back against an ancient old oak.

He took in several deep breaths as his gaze scanned the area directly around him. His heart seemed to stop as he saw one of his men lying prone on the grass. Dead?

He crouched and ran to the man's side. Burt. Not dead, but unconscious. He'd been taken down with an obvious struggle and Tanner had a feeling that Burt wasn't the only man down. Somehow the rebels had managed to sneak up on the guards and take them down soundlessly, one by one.

He gazed back toward the house, fighting rage as he thought of his men. There…on the side of the house, a man stood near the window of one of the spare bedrooms. The faint moonlight glittered off the barrel of the gun he held as he crept closer to the window, apparently attempting to see inside.

These men had been sent to kill Anna. Tanner knew he had to take them on one by one to have any chance at all. With this in mind, he moved quickly across the lawn as the man lowered his gun to peer into the window.

Without boots and only in his bare feet, Tanner moved soundlessly against the thick, springy grass. He came up behind the man, wrapped a forearm around his neck and squeezed as tight as he could. He pulled tight, cutting off air.

A grunt escaped the man as he struggled against Tanner's hold. It took only seconds for Tanner to render the man unconscious.

As he slipped to the ground, Tanner quickly duct-taped his wrists and ankles, then slapped several pieces of the sticky tape over his mouth. He grabbed him by the feet and dragged him across the lawn and into the trees.

One down, and he had no idea how many were left. Where was his backup? At that moment he heard a grunt come from the trees nearby and he hoped the sound meant he was no longer battling alone.

Moving stealthily in a couched position he made his way through the trees. He knew the landscape as well as he knew his own name. That was his advantage as he stalked his prey through the woods.

There was little noise. The crickets and other insects were silent, as if sensing danger. The only sound was the faint slap of footsteps against grass and an occasional snap of a twig.

He followed the sounds until he spied his quarry, another burly male moving like a shadow in the night. He was moving toward the opposite side of the house from where Tanner had caught up with the other man.

Movement on his left made him jerk his head, and he saw Zack slicing through the trees with speed and agility, obviously tracking somebody.

Tanner looked back toward the house and froze. He'd momentarily lost sight of the man who had been near the house. His pulse raced as he tried to find the assassin.

He heard the bullet before he felt the impact. The faint puff of a gun with a silencer. The bullet ripped into the bark of a tree mere inches from his head. He threw himself to the ground.

Game on.

If he'd been coldly emotionless before, he was positively bloodless now. This was survival. Another bullet hit the tree just above where he lay on the ground. He rolled to the left, came up to his feet and ran for the cover of the nearest tree trunk.

The flash of the last shot had let him know where the enemy was hiding, and Tanner moved farther into the woods, hoping to come up behind the man.

Slowly and steadily he moved. He still had a visual of the shooter and knew from the way the man turned his head from side to side, gun pointed first one direction then another, that the man had lost sight of him.

He only hoped that while he was taking care of this threat some of the other men were watching the front of the house to assure nobody got inside. He was comforted only by the fact that if anyone tried to get into the bathroom where Anna was hiding, she'd scream bloody murder and alert him to her danger.

With the silence of a shadow Tanner moved toward the gunman, grateful when a cloud drifted in front of the moon, momentarily obscuring everything. He used the cover of the deep darkness to move closer.

When the cloud drifted away and moonlight once again filtered down, he found himself no more than twenty feet behind the gunman.

It would be easy to take a shot now, to eliminate the threat with a bullet, but he was afraid the sound of the gunshot would rally any others he might not have seen. He had no idea how many more might be hiding in the woods, concealed by the darkness.

He'd much prefer to take the man down soundlessly, as he had the first one. With this thought in mind, he crept closer, careful not to make a sound that would give away his position.

When he was close enough that he could smell the body odor emanating from the man, could hear his slightly raspy breaths, he lunged forward and knocked the gun from the man's hand.

Before he could get a choke hold around his neck, the man spun around and clipped Tanner in the jaw with his fist.

The blow landed squarely. Pain shot through the side of his head. He ignored the pain and thrust a fist into the man's stomach. The man gasped and stumbled backward. Tanner gave him no time to recover, but hit him again, this time with an uppercut that snapped his head upward.

The man lunged forward, swinging wildly, and again a fist clipped Tanner's jaw. With all the force his body could summon, Tanner threw a punch and connected once again with the man's stomach.

The man fell to the ground, grasping for the gun that had fallen into the grass. Tanner grabbed his feet to pull him away from the gun, then fell on top of him and wrapped his arm around his neck. As he pulled with his arm, he pushed at the back of the head with his other hand.

Unconsciousness came quickly. Gasping for breath, Tanner rose and bound the man's hands and feet with the duct tape. As he tore off a piece of the tape to slap across the man's mouth a roar split the night, a roar followed by the whoosh of flames.

He looked toward the house and in horror saw that

it appeared to be consumed by flames. Glass exploded outward from all the windows.

"Anna!" he screamed, and ran toward the inferno.

She heard the explosion, but remained in the bathroom, afraid to move, afraid to ignore Tanner's order that she remain in the bathroom until he returned for her.

She stood in the dark, in the tub, wondering what was happening. Other than the explosion, she'd heard not a sound since she'd run to hide. What had caused the loud blast? What was going on outside?

Tanner. Her heart cried out. Please, please, keep him safe. Please let him be okay. At least she hadn't heard any gunshots. That was something, wasn't it? At least she knew he probably hadn't been shot.

She stared in the direction of the locked door, able to see it only a little from the moonlight drifting in through the window high above the tub. She was afraid who might enter.

It took her a moment to realize she smelled something...something acrid...something burning. She heard the faint tinkle of glass breaking somewhere in the house. The smell grew stronger, more pronounced.

Smoke! It burned her eyes, tickled the back of her throat. She coughed. Once. Twice. A spasm of choking left her weakly leaning against the bathroom wall.

Needing light, she reached her hand out and flipped the switch, shocked to see the thick black smoke pouring into the room from under the door.

Fire! The house was on fire. She shoved a fist in her mouth to staunch the scream that threatened to escape. She had to get out. She couldn't wait for Tanner. It wouldn't take long for her to die from smoke inhalation.

She jumped out of the tub and grabbed hold of the doorknob. Instantly she yanked her hand back. Hot. The knob was like grabbing hold of a hot chunk of coal. She couldn't go out that way. Smoke poured in beneath the door, and she quickly wet a towel and shoved it against the door to stop the flow of smoke.

She stepped back into the tub and gazed at the window overhead. It was a small window, up high over the tub. She could grab the edge with her fingertips, but didn't think she'd be able to pull herself up and through.

She shrieked as the lights went off, leaving her only with a sliver of moonlight for light and the thickening smoke that made it difficult to breathe.

A fit of coughing sent her to her knees. Where was Tanner? Had the rebels killed him? A piercing pain shot through her at the thought. Please don't let him be dead, she mentally prayed as another coughing spasm overtook her.

She was losing it. She felt the blackness closing in. The air was too thick to breathe and she could barely keep her eyes open. In the faint moonlight the smoke thickened and boiled around her.

*Let go,* a little voice whispered in her head. *Just a few deep breaths and you'll go to sleep.*

Just her luck, to finally find the love she'd yearned for, then die when it was still fresh and new in her heart.

*Just breathe, it will all be over soon.* The little voice in her head was an irritating refrain. But she'd never been a quitter, and between sobs and coughs she slid from the tub and tried to find something she could use to break the window. If she could just get some air, she'd be fine.

Again the darkness threatened, but before it could claim her completely, the bathroom door burst open and Tanner came in. He said nothing, but pulled her from the floor and lifted her up over his shoulder and ran.

She was vaguely aware of the fire all around them, but all she could think about was the fact that Tanner had lied to her. He'd told her a cowboy threw a woman over his shoulder when he loved her. But he didn't love her. This was the last conscious thought she had.

# Chapter 13

Anna awakened to the early-morning sun seeping softly through the window. She started to sit up, worried that she'd be late for breakfast and Smokey would give her attitude. But she wasn't at the ranch. She blinked and looked around, for a moment disoriented.

It was a hospital room. She didn't move as her mind raced. Why was she here? She didn't seem to be hurt, other than a bad sore throat.

The fire. The smoke. Her memory returned with a jolt. But she remembered nothing after Tanner breaking into the bathroom, nothing of how she had come to be here and what had happened.

She was alone in the room, although the door was

open and she saw that somebody was seated just out-side. "Hello?" Her voice was husky and she winced, wishing for a drink of water to ease the burning ache.

It was Tanner seated just outside her room. He jumped up and walked in, the sight of him both joy-ous and painful at the same time.

She was thrilled that he appeared to be all right, but the sight of him reminded her of all that would never be. She loved him and he didn't love her back.

"Hi." For the first time since she'd met him he sounded hesitant…tentative, although his facial expression was, as usual, inscrutable. "How are you doing?"

"Thirsty," she croaked.

She watched as he poured her a glass of water from a pitcher on the stand next to the bed. He stuck in a straw then held the glass to her lips so she could take a sip.

The cold water soothed the scratchiness of her throat, but did nothing to ease the ache that filled her heart. She needed something, anything, to take her mind away from the memory of the painful conversa-tion they'd had before he'd spied movement outside the window.

She desperately wanted to think about anything other than the fact that Tanner didn't love her, that there was no future here for her with him. "What happened?" she asked.

He pulled up a chair next to her bed and sat, his

gaze somber. For the first time she noticed the slight purple bruise that decorated his left jaw. "Looks like you lost the battle."

He reached up and touched his jaw, then shrugged. "Maybe lost the battle, but won the war. You should see the other guy." He leaned back in the chair. "There were three of them. I managed to take out two, but while I was fighting with the second man, a third somehow got to the front of the house and threw some sort of small bomb through the window. The explosion brought my men from the main house. They caught the third man and all three are now in custody down at the sheriff's office."

She struggled to sit up and he quickly jumped out of the chair to plump the pillow behind her. "Thanks," she murmured as he once again sat in the chair. "I know I'm in a hospital, but where?"

"Cotter Creek Memorial," he replied. A faint whisper of a smile curved the corners of his lips. "A big name for a small, twenty-bed facility."

She had a feeling he was hoping for a returning smile from her, but she simply couldn't summon one. "Why am I here? I don't seem to be hurt."

Any kind of a smile disappeared as a grim look thinned his lips. "You inhaled a lot of smoke. By the time I got you outside you were unconscious. You came around a bit in the ambulance that brought you here, but the doctor sedated you after you were breathing normally. He wanted to keep you overnight for observation."

She closed her eyes, remembering those moments when the bathroom had filled with choking smoke, the feel of the hot doorknob in her fingers, the absolute terror that had gripped her. If not for Tanner she would be dead.

She opened her eyes and gazed at him, wishing she could be the one to put soothing compresses against his bruised jaw, lay a cool hand across his weary-looking forehead.

"I know you were just doing your job, but thank you for saving my life."

"It's what I do," he replied, averting his gaze from hers.

She closed her eyes again, but only for a moment. As she thought of the consequence of that smoke, that heat, her eyelids popped open and she gasped. "Your home?" she asked, even though she was afraid she knew the answer.

"Was just a place of lumber and nails. It can all be rebuilt." His voice was steady, without emotion.

"Oh, Tanner. I'm so sorry." Tears burned at her eyes as she thought of the house he'd been working on for the past three years. Now, all gone, nothing but ash and memories.

"Hey, no tears allowed," he replied gently. "I was well aware of the risk I took when I brought you into the house."

"I'm sure you didn't expect your house to burn to the ground," she retorted.

"Anna, I'm just glad you're safe."

"Of course, I wouldn't want to be a blot on your perfect protection record." She hadn't meant the bitterness to creep into her voice, but it had.

He stood, his gaze drifting away from her face and toward the bank of windows. "I've got some good news for you. I heard from your father this morning. We've set up a meet early tomorrow."

"At the ranch?" she asked.

"No, the ranch has been compromised. We're meeting him twenty miles from here, at a small convenience store off the highway." His gaze found hers again. "Within twenty-four hours you'll be gone from this dusty little cowboy town and back to the lifestyle you were accustomed to living.

It was as if they hadn't had their conversation in bed the night before, the conversation where she'd told him of the changes she intended to make in her life.

Apparently he hadn't believed her. It didn't matter whether he did or not. She knew what she wanted to do, with or without Tanner West.

"When can I get out of here?" she asked.

"The doctor said he'd probably release you sometime this morning. I'll go see if I can find him and get some information for you."

He seemed relieved, relieved to leave the room, relieved that her father was coming and that his time with her was coming to an end.

As he left the room Anna turned her head toward

the window where the morning had brightened, portending a beautiful day.

Her last day in Cotter Creek.

Her last day with Tanner West.

She'd spent all the years since she'd turned eighteen running from the loneliness that had no name, the yearning for something nebulous and undefined.

Her loneliness now had a name…Tanner West. She knew he was exactly what she'd yearned for, what she'd wanted, needed in her life.

Unfortunately he didn't want or need her.

The doctor released Anna just before noon and the drive back to the ranch was a silent one. The past twelve hours had been the longest in Tanner's life.

When he'd seen the flames licking up to the sky and had known that Anna was inside the inferno, a desperation the likes of which he'd never known had flooded him. Both his father and Zack had tried to keep him from going inside the house, but no force on earth could have stopped him.

As the ranch hands wrestled the assassin to the ground, Tanner had broken away and run around the house to the back door. The fire had been intense, but thankfully had been mostly confined to the living room.

When he'd broken in the bathroom door and seen Anna on her hands and knees gasping for air, he'd felt as if he'd been unable to breathe.

Throughout the night as she had slept in the hospital room, he'd sat in a chair just outside her door, making sure that nothing and nobody could harm her.

Disaster had been so close…too close. He'd nearly lost her, and as he drove toward the ranch his mind played and replayed all the decisions he had made concerning her safety from the moment she'd charged into the office.

Had he made mistakes? Had he allowed his desire to be with Anna to cloud his judgment? He didn't know. The one thing he did know was that if they'd lingered in bed after making love, if he'd been 100 percent focused on her during the argument they'd had, he would have missed that shadow moving in front of the window. In all probability both of them would now be dead.

Even knowing he'd probably made mistakes, understanding that he'd crossed a boundary and had gotten too personally involved, he still wanted to take her in his arms and hold her tight. Even though he knew it was the worst possible thing to do, he wanted to wrap her in his arms and kiss the sadness from her lips.

Instead he tightened his hands on the steering wheel and scowled out the window, aware of her sad gaze lingering on him. Behind his truck was another vehicle holding two armed men in Tanner's employment. Even though they had successfully thwarted one attack, that didn't mean the danger had passed. Tanner hadn't been willing to take any chances. He'd had guards outside her hospital room and would have the house heavily guarded for the night.

"Did you have insurance on the house?" she asked, breaking the uncomfortable silence that had existed since the moment they'd gotten into his truck.

"Yeah. Don't worry about it. It will all be taken care of." He glanced over at her, noting that despite the trauma of the night's events, she looked lovely.

She was clad in a pair of sweatpants and a T-shirt that a nurse had offered her so she wouldn't have to go home in her smoky clothing. The sweatpants were too big and the T-shirt swam on her, but still she was as pretty as Tanner had ever seen her. So pretty it ached deep inside him.

It was a good thing her father would arrive tomorrow. It was the best thing for both of them. She might not realize it at the moment, but she needed something different than he could give her. She deserved more than he was willing to give.

He was relieved when the ranch house came into sight. He'd been afraid that at any moment she might want to resume the discussion they'd been having before all hell had broken loose. He didn't want to revisit it. There was nothing more to say between them except goodbye.

Red and Smokey came out to the front porch as if they'd been standing inside watching for their arrival.

Both men approached the passenger door as Tanner came to a stop.

"Come on, I got some herbal tea waiting for you," Smokey said.

"And I got some magazines for you at the grocery store, some of those fashion women-kind magazines so you can read and relax while you recover," Red added.

For moment Tanner thought she might burst into tears, but instead she pulled herself out of the car and with the dignity he'd come to expect from her, walked toward the house, flanked by the two older men.

Tanner saw with satisfaction that the house was surrounded by armed men. He'd arranged for additional men that morning, taking no chance that they wouldn't be prepared for another attack of some kind.

The air still held the faint tinge of smoke, a reminder of just how close he'd come to losing her last night. He was about to follow them inside when Zack called to him.

He and Zack had really not spoken much at all since the day Zack had returned from his assignment and as Zack approached him, Tanner felt his heart constrict with emotions too great to bear.

"You doing okay?" Zack asked. There was still a haunted look in his eyes and again Tanner wondered what had happened between his brother and the client who had been killed.

"I'm fine. What about you? We haven't really had a chance to talk."

Zack looked off in the distance, a frown creasing his forehead. "I love you, Tanner, but you aren't always the easiest man in the world to talk to."

Tanner shoved his hands into his pockets and sucked in a deep breath. "Why is that?"

Zack looked at him once again. "I'm not sure. Maybe it's because I get the feeling you never allow yourself to get personally involved in any situation. You don't give much of yourself and that makes it hard for anyone to want to give to you."

"I'm sorry." He didn't know what else to say.

Zack shrugged. "It's all right." He paused a long moment but Tanner had the feeling he wasn't finished speaking yet. "You look at her differently than I've ever seen you look at anyone." The words were soft and once again Zack averted his gaze from his brother's. "She looks at you the same way."

A knot formed in Tanner's chest. He wanted to protest, to tell his brother that he was mistaken, but he knew he'd only sound the fool. "She's leaving tomorrow." The knot expanded in his chest. "Her father's due to arrive sometime tomorrow morning."

"That's what I heard. How do you feel about that?"

Feel? How did he feel about it? He'd spent every moment since the phone call from King Bjorn trying not to think about it, not to feel at all. "It's time," he replied succinctly.

For a moment the two brothers remained side by side, staring off in the distance where Tanner's house was nothing more than a rubble of still smoldering ash and concrete.

"Did you love her?" Tanner asked abruptly.

Zack flashed him a quick glance, then returned his gaze to the distance. "Not like a lover. I loved her but not in a romantic way." He took a tremulous deep breath. "We became close as friends. Melissa was a wonderful woman and so easy to talk to. She told me about the heartache of her marriage and I found myself telling her all about my relationship with Jamie."

Jamie Coffer was a young woman Zack had dated nearly two years before. Everyone had just assumed the two of them would be married, but Jamie had left town and within months had married another man.

Tanner had no idea what had caused the breakup and until this moment hadn't realized that apparently the whole thing had left some deep scars on Zack's heart.

"I'm sorry, Zack." Zack turned to look at him once again. "I'm sorry if I haven't been the brother you needed." The words came with difficulty, but he knew they were words that needed to be said. "I always wanted to be there for you, for you and all the rest of us kids."

"I don't know if you've noticed or not, brother, but we're all grown up now. Maybe you need to ease up a little and figure out where you're going in your life."

Tanner frowned, realizing that Zack's words almost echoed what Anna had said to him the night before. Where was he going with his life? He was thirty-five years old and even though he'd told himself over and over again that he eventually wanted a wife and a family, he'd done nothing to take steps to achieve that particular goal.

"I'd better get inside to check on her highness," he finally said.

"Just one thing to think about," Zack said. "I think I'd rather take a chance at getting my heart broken than live the rest of my life with regrets. What about you?"

Tanner didn't reply, knew his brother expected no reply. Instead he turned and went into the house. Life seemed to have turned upside down.

Smokey was making herbal tea and his thirty-one-year-old brother seemed to be trying to give him advice. For the first time in his life Tanner felt as if he'd lost control and it scared him.

He found his father and Smokey in the kitchen with Anna, who was seated at the table, a cup of tea in front of her. Her face was pale, her eyes lifeless as she stared listlessly out the window.

Was it the trauma of the night's events that had sucked all the life, all the energy, from her? Or was it him? Surely it was the fact that she'd nearly lost her life to smoke inhalation and nothing more.

"I made some soup and sandwiches for lunch," Smokey said. "I figured we'd eat informally right here."

Another surprise. Smokey usually insisted on eating properly in the dining room. The old man smiled at Anna. "I made some special chicken soup. Nothing better for a sore throat no matter what made it sore in the first place."

Special tea…special soup. It appeared Anna had made an indelible mark on the heart of Smokey. Amazing, Tanner thought as he sat across from her at the table. How had a princess who had been in the house only a mere week managed to affect each and every person who lived here?

"I hate to be the bearer of more bad news," Red said as they began to eat lunch.

"What bad news?" Tanner asked.

"I heard that Gray Sampson died this morning."

Shock swept through Tanner. "How? What happened?"

"Seems he got thrown from his horse, hit his head on a rock and was killed."

"Damn, that's the second accidental death in the last couple of months." Tanner frowned. Two months ago Joe Wainfield had been killed in his field in a freak tractor accident.

"This Gray Sampson, he was a friend of yours?" Anna's features radiated concern as she gazed at him.

"He lives on a ranch on the north side of town. He was a respected rancher." Tanner looked down at his plate. He didn't want to see that caring in her eyes, that empathetic softness that threatened to pull him in.

She'd be gone tomorrow, Tanner told himself as he

ate. Then everything would get back to normal. He could get back to normal.

He needed to get back to the office, back to working long days so the nights seemed shorter. He needed to get back to focusing solely on the business, so there wouldn't be time to recognize and acknowledge his loneliness.

He was grateful when the meal was over and Anna retreated to her room for a nap. Red headed for the front door and Tanner remained at the kitchen table watching while Smokey cleared the dishes from lunch.

"You look like you sat on a thornbush," Smokey observed as he grabbed the plates in front of Tanner. "Something wrong?"

"Just wondering if the danger is over."

"Even if it's not, you've got enough men stationed around the house to stop any kind of attack that might come," Smokey said. "Besides, from what I heard, one of the half-dozen men Jim arrested last night is singing, and his tune is that there was just their team sent to assassinate the king and Anna."

"I hope he is singing a song of truth," Tanner replied dryly. "I won't relax until Anna and her father are far, far away from here." He stood. "I've got some work to do in the office. I'll be in there if anyone needs anything."

Smokey grunted and Tanner left the kitchen. As he sank down at the desk in the office, he felt a comforting familiarity wash over him. This was where he belonged, taking care of business, not thinking about the woman in the bedroom who had momentarily twisted his world upside down.

Within twenty-four hours she'd be gone and he tried to tell himself that was a good thing.

## Chapter 14

Anna stood at her bedroom window for a last good-bye to the place where she'd come to love. The sun was just rising, painting the landscape in lush tones of pinks and oranges.

Although she was eager to see her father, her eagerness was tempered with the overwhelming grief that after today she would never see Tanner again. After today she'd never see his frowns, or the beauty of his smiles. She'd never again hear his smooth deep voice. She'd never again taste the passion of his kisses.

In her twenty-five years she'd dated enough men to recognize the man she wanted to spend the rest of her life with—the man who didn't want to spend his life with her.

Sleep had been elusive the night before. She'd tossed and turned, playing and replaying every moment she'd spent with Tanner. What she'd wanted to do was to sneak into his bedroom to make love with him one final time before they parted forever, but she'd been afraid that if she did that she'd never recover. It was difficult enough as it was.

She'd already packed what little she would take with her. She was taking only her small overnight bag, her red boots and the pair of jeans and T-shirt that she wore. The rest of the things Tanner had bought for her she was leaving behind…along with her heart.

"Anna, it's time to go." Tanner's voice spoke from the doorway.

She stood reluctantly and carried the overnight bag into the living room, dropped it on the floor, then went into the kitchen where Red and Smokey sat at the table.

"I want to thank you for your hospitality," she said to Red. "Thank you for opening your home to me during this difficult time."

Red jumped up out of his chair and took her hand in his. "It's been an honor, Anna. I'd forgotten how nice it was to have a female presence in the house." He dropped her hand with a sad smile.

She went over to where Smokey sat, looking as grumpy as she'd ever seen him. She didn't let his crabby look stop her from planting a fond kiss on his forehead. "Thank you, Smokey."

"For what?" He snorted. "I didn't do nothing special. I wouldn't even change your sheets on your bed for you."

She smiled at him, her heart feeling as if it was far too big for her chest. "You'll never know what you did for me." She looked at Red. "Neither of you will ever know just how much you have given me in the time I've been here." She felt tears burning too close to the surface. She swallowed hard against them.

"I just hope you find what you're looking for," Smokey said softly.

I did, she wanted to say. I did, but it didn't work out.

"We need to go," Tanner said, his voice tense.

Three guards awaited her on the porch and they surrounded her as she and Tanner made their way to his pickup truck.

She shouldn't be thinking of this as the end of something, but rather as the beginning…the beginning of a new life for her.

She should be excited and eagerly anticipating what the future might bring. But as she slid into the passenger seat her heart didn't feel the anticipation of new beginnings. It felt only the pain of the ending of something wonderful…magical.

As Tanner got behind the steering wheel, he checked his watch. "We're to meet your father in thirty minutes." He waited for a car to pull in front of him and behind him. Apparently he was still taking her safety very seriously.

"There was no way we could have your father meet us at the ranch," he said once they were on their way. "This location has been compromised. The convenience store where we're meeting him is off the beaten path and I've already sent three men ahead to secure the location before we arrive. I'm sure you're eager to see your father again."

She nodded, too heart weary to summon any kind of reply. Yes, she'd be glad to see her father again, but she wasn't returning to Niflheim anytime in the near future even if the unrest there was resolved. She couldn't return to the place that had never really been her home, a lifestyle that had only deepened the ache in her heart.

If she was certain about anything, it was that her future didn't include Niflheim.

They spent the rest of the short journey in silence. Anna felt too sick to speak, knowing that each and every mile took her closer to her final goodbye to Tanner.

They arrived at the convenience store ahead of King Bjorn. Tanner's men were already there, stationed around the perimeter. Anna unfastened her seat belt and realized she wanted to say goodbye to Tanner here and now, while they were alone.

"Tanner."

He turned to face her with those beautiful dark

green eyes and those strong, stern features that she'd grown to love. The corner of his mouth twitched, and with that slight tick of vulnerability she found the words she wanted, needed to say.

"I love you, Tanner. I won't say it again, because I've said it enough that I'd hoped you'd believe the words. But, there is something I want to tell you. During some talks with Smokey I was introduced to a very special woman."

He frowned with obvious confusion. "I don't understand."

She leaned toward him and saw the corner of his mouth twitch once again. "Smokey told me about a lovely woman, a strong woman who had the world by the tail. She might have become wealthy, she might have married royalty and become a princess or even a queen. She might have done all kinds of things to bring herself wealth and adulation, but she chose to marry the man she loved and have his children. Smokey told me about your mother, Tanner, and that's the kind of woman I hope to be."

There was a flash of genuine pain in his eyes. "Anna, for God's sake, don't make this any more difficult than it already is."

She leaned even closer and could smell him, that familiar scent of sunshine and wind, of faint cologne and male. God help her, but it smelled like home.

"I just needed to tell you one last thing," she continued. "If you don't love me, then you're doing the right thing by allowing me to leave here. But if you do love me, it would be a tragic mistake on your part to let me go."

At that moment two cars approached the convenience store and Anna knew her father had arrived. It was time to go.

The two cars pulled to a halt. The first men out of the car were armed and obviously there for protection. The third man out was Anna's father.

King Bjorn Johansson was a big man. Standing well over six feet tall, he had a broad girth that spoke of good living. Despite his large size, he carried himself with a regal grace and a commanding dignity.

Anna got out of Tanner's truck and flew to her father's arms, vaguely aware of another imposing man getting out of her father's car.

"Ah, my dear. I knew Mr. West would take good care of you," he said as he released her. "He's a man like his father." He smiled over her head at Tanner.

Tanner returned the smile with a respectful bow. "It will take years for me to be the man my father is."

"I understand there was trouble last night and you lost your home."

Anna felt herself lost as her father focused all his attention on Tanner. Her resolve to make a future all her own grew. She adored her father, but would she always be dismissed by him as something pretty and frivolous?

"A little trouble and nothing that insurance won't cover," Tanner replied as he gestured for the king to move inside the store. He wasn't comfortable standing out in the open despite the guards that surrounded them.

"Mr. West, may I introduce you to General Jorge Hauptman," King Bjorn said once they were inside the store. He gestured to the dignified man standing just behind him.

Anna watched as Tanner and general Hauptman shook hands. "Father, what is the news from Niflheim?" she asked.

"At this moment General Hauptman's troops are attempting to wrest control of the palace from the rebel forces who hold it."

"And you expect this to be successful?" Anna asked. Even though she had no intention of returning, her heart ached with the divisiveness that had ripped apart the small country.

General Hauptman nodded. "John Swenson and his Brotherhood of the Mist used surprise and an alarming lack of security to overwhelm the palace, much like what the terrorists did here in your country on 9/11. But the Brotherhood of the Mist is a small, rather disorganized group. We hope to have the palace back in our control by nightfall."

King Bjorn looked at Tanner. "General Hauptman and I have been at odds in the past. But he has agreed to work with me in a strong, unified front."

"Certainly the danger has not passed and will not be over even when we gain control of the palace," Hauptman added.

"But it's my country," King Bjorn said passionately. "And no matter what the dangers, it is where I belong."

"What about the men who were arrested here last night?" Tanner asked.

"They will be transported back to Niflheim to stand trail for treason. Unfortunately we have no way of knowing if there are others in the country. I would hope that after today you and your family will be safe."

"It's Anna's safety I'm concerned about," Tanner replied, but he kept his gaze focused on the king and not on Anna.

"Anna will have all the bodyguards she needs to assure her safety in Niflheim," he said. "As I said before, we're quite aware that dangerous times lie ahead and we will take the necessary precautions to ward off tragedy. We will not be caught unaware and unprepared again."

Anna said nothing, aware that now wasn't the time to tell her father that she had very different plans for herself. She had no intention of returning to Niflheim and living with armed guards." Surely a princess could find obscurity and happiness in the United States.

"And now we must be on our way," King Bjorn said.

"We have a flight to catch this afternoon and many plans to make in the meantime." He held out his hand to Tanner.

Anna watched the two men in her life shake hands, and again tears threatened to fall. Tanner—her heart cried—I don't want to say goodbye!

"Ready?" her father asked.

She nodded and picked up the overnight bag that Tanner had carried with him into the store. Flanked by bodyguards, she and her father and the general left the convenience store.


"Somebody want to tell me what's going on?" The ready voice belonged to the teenage male working the counter. His eyes were huge and his protruding Adam's apple danced up and down.

"Don't worry about it, kid," Tanner said, then turned his attention out the window.

His heart hurt as Anna's final private words to him went around and around in his head, mingling with Zack's advice about regrets.

He hadn't meant to fall in love with Anna. He hadn't meant to ever fall in love with anyone. Love hurt too much. He'd learned that lesson with his mother's death, and at that time he'd done exactly what Anna had accused him of doing…built fences around his heart.

But now, the fences were tumbling down and raw emotion swept through him. Would he be satisfied living forever with regrets or was he man enough to face his fear and go after what he wanted more than anything else in the world?

Anna. Her name cried out from his heart. Anna, with her flashing blue eyes and sparkling blond hair. Anna, with her sweet lips and womanly curves. She intoxicated him.

Anna, with her determination to be something more, with her sense of humor and warm laughter. She already held his heart in her hands. So, what was he waiting for?

He watched her get into the back seat of the second car with her father and energy ripped through him. He tore open the store's door and raced outside as the roar of their engines sounded.

"Wait!" He ran to the car that held the king and his daughter and pounded on the window. He saw Anna's face through the window, her eyes huge and her mouth forming an O of surprise. He ripped open her door and stared at her.

"Don't go." The words tore from his throat, a desperate plea like he'd never voiced before.

He'd expected her to bolt out of the car and into his arms, but instead she remained seated, staring at him with those gorgeous eyes. "Why not?" she asked. She waited only a moment, then continued. "You have to say the words, Tanner. I need to hear the words."

"I love you. I love you, Anna, and I can't imagine my life without you." Once the dam had burst, the words seemed to come without thought, driven out of him by sheer emotion. "I need you to make me laugh. I need you to remind me that there's more to life than work. Anna, I need you to help me be the man I want to be. And I'll help you be the woman you want to be."

Tears filled her eyes and for a dreadful moment he wondered if he was too late or if perhaps she'd realized her love for him wasn't real after all. "You heard what my father said. There might still be danger."

"Then I won't just be your husband—I'll be your lifetime bodyguard," he replied. His heart hammered as she leaned to the side and said something to her father. Then she turned back to Tanner, and in the smile she gave him he saw his future.

She stepped out of the car and set her overnight bag on the ground. He started to take her into his arms, needing her close, wanting to embrace her forever, but she held up a hand to stop him. "Throw me over your shoulder, Tanner."

"Excuse me?"

Her eyes flashed with the impatience he'd come to love. "You heard me—throw me over your shoulder."

"Why would you want me to do that?" he asked.

She smiled, her charming dimples flashing. "Because that's what cowboys do when they love a woman."

With a burst of laughter that seemed to fill his very soul, he grabbed her and lifted her over his shoulder, then bent and picked up her overnight case.

"She'll be in touch," he said to a surprised-looking but smiling King Bjorn, then turned to carry her to his pickup truck. The men who had been tapped for guard duty clapped and cheered, and in that sound Tanner heard his future calling.

# INTIMATE MOMENTS™

presents a provocative new miniseries by
award-winning author

# INGRID WEAVER

# PAYBACK

Three rebels were brought back from the brink and
recruited into the shadowy Payback Organization.
In return for this extraordinary second chance, they
must each repay one favor in the future. But if they
renege on their promise, everything that matters
will be ripped away...including love!

**Available in March 2005:**

## The Angel and the Outlaw
(IM #1352)

Hayley Tavistock will do anything to avenge the
murder of her brother—including forming an
uneasy alliance with gruff ex-con Cooper Webb.
With the walls closing in around them, can love
defy the odds?

**Watch for Book #2 in June 2005...**

## Loving the Lone Wolf
(IM #1370)

*Available at your favorite retail outlet.*

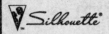

If you enjoyed what you just read,
then we've got an offer you can't resist!

# Take 2 bestselling love stories FREE!

# Plus get a FREE surprise gift!

**Clip this page and mail it to Silhouette Reader Service™**

| IN U.S.A. | IN CANADA |
|---|---|
| 3010 Walden Ave. | P.O. Box 609 |
| P.O. Box 1867 | Fort Erie, Ontario |
| Buffalo, N.Y. 14240-1867 | L2A 5X3 |

**YES!** Please send me 2 free Silhouette Intimate Moments® novels and my free surprise gift. After receiving them, if I don't wish to receive anymore, I can return the shipping statement marked cancel. If I don't cancel, I will receive 6 brand-new novels every month, before they're available in stores! In the U.S.A., bill me at the bargain price of $4.24 plus 25¢ shipping and handling per book and applicable sales tax, if any*. In Canada, bill me at the bargain price of $4.99 plus 25¢ shipping and handling per book and applicable taxes**. That's the complete price and a savings of at least 10% off the cover prices—what a great deal! I understand that accepting the 2 free books and gift places me under no obligation ever to buy any books. I can always return a shipment and cancel at any time. Even if I never buy another book from Silhouette, the 2 free books and gift are mine to keep forever.

245 SDN DZ9A
345 SDN DZ9C

| Name | (PLEASE PRINT) | |
|---|---|---|
| Address | Apt.# | |
| City | State/Prov. | Zip/Postal Code |

*Not valid to current Silhouette Intimate Moments® subscribers.*

*Want to try two free books from another series?*
*Call 1-800-873-8635 or visit www.morefreebooks.com.*

\* Terms and prices subject to change without notice. Sales tax applicable in N.Y.
\*\* Canadian residents will be charged applicable provincial taxes and GST.
   All orders subject to approval. Offer limited to one per household].
   ® are registered trademarks owned and used by the trademark owner and or its licensee.

INMOM04R                    ©2004 Harlequin Enterprises Limited

# SPECIAL EDITION™

Introducing a brand-new miniseries by
Silhouette Special Edition favorite author
Marie Ferrarella

One special necklace,
three charm-filled romances!

# BECAUSE A HUSBAND
# IS FOREVER

### by Marie Ferrarella
Available March 2005
Silhouette Special Edition #1671

Dakota Delany had always wanted a marriage like
the one her parents had, but after she found her
fiancé cheating, she gave up on love. When her
radio talk show came up with the idea of having her
spend two weeks with hunky bodyguard Ian Russell,
she protested—until she discovered she wanted Ian
to continue guarding her body forever!

*Available at your favorite retail outlet.*

*Where love comes alive™*

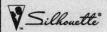

# INTIMATE MOMENTS™

Don't miss the eerie
Intimate Moments debut
by

# MARGARET CARTER

## Embracing Darkness

Linnet Carroll's life was perfectly ordinary
and admittedly rather boring—until
she crossed paths with Max Tremayne.
The seductive and mysterious Max
claimed to be a 500-year-old vampire…
and Linnet believed him. Romance ignited
as they joined together to hunt down
the renegade vampire responsible for
the deaths of Max's brother and Linnet's
niece. But even if they succeeded, would
fate ever give this mismatched couple a
future together?

***Available March 2005
at your favorite retail outlet.***

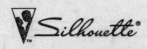

# COMING NEXT MONTH

**#1351 SECOND-CHANCE HERO—Justine Davis**
*Redstone, Incorporated*
Called to a crime-ridden tropical island, Redstone security chief
John Draven was reunited with Grace O'Conner, a single mother
recuperating from a devastating loss. Memories of what had happened
to this woman, what *he* had done to her, haunted him. When Grace's life
was put in jeopardy, would Draven be able to save her…again?

**#1352 THE ANGEL AND THE OUTLAW—Ingrid Weaver**
*Payback*
Grief-stricken Hayley Tavistock would do anything to avenge the
murder of her brother, a decorated cop. But she needed the help
of Cooper Webb, the hard-edged former thief who had his own
desperate reasons for pursuing this case with a vengeance. As sparks
and unanswered questions flew between them, Cooper and Hayley
were determined to find the killer before he struck again.…

**#1353 HER SECRET AGENT MAN—Cindy Dees**
*Charlie Squad*
To force banker Julia Ferrare into laundering money, her sister had been
taken hostage—by their father. Julia begged Charlie Squad, an elite Air
Force Special Forces team, for help. But she had a secret she needed to
hide from Dutch, the sinfully handsome agent sent to meet her. Once the
truth was revealed, would Dutch ever be able to forgive her?

**#1354 STRANDED WITH A STRANGER—Frances Housden**
*International Affairs*
Wealthy, pampered Chelsea Tedman never expected to be climbing
Mount Everest with a mysterious, alluring stranger. But only rugged
guide Kurt Jellic could get her up the cursed mountain to solve the
mystery of her sister's fatal fall. Would hidden dangers and passions
drive them into each other's arms…or plunge them to their own icy
demise?

**#1355 EMBRACING DARKNESS—Margaret Carter**
Until she met Max Tremayne, Linnet Carroll had led an ordinary
existence. But Max claimed to be a 500-year-old vampire…and
Linnet believed him. Now they needed to join together to hunt down the
renegade vampire responsible for the deaths of Max's brother and
Linnet's niece. Even if they succeeded, would this mismatched couple
ever be able to have a life together?

**#1356 WORTH EVERY RISK—Dianna Love Snell**
Branded with a wrongful conviction, Angel Farentino intended to prove
her innocence or die trying. As she ran for her life, she didn't need a
sexy savior distracting her. But undercover DEA agent Zane Jackson
had his own secrets—like discovering whether Angel was guilty of a
felony, or just guilty of stealing his heart. To find out, he needed to keep
her alive…a mission worth every risk.

SIMCNM0205